# A RIVER OF STONES

# Books by Kathryn Elizabeth Jones

A River of Stones

## Parable Series

Conquering Your Goliaths: A Parable of the Five Stones

Conquering Your Goliaths: Guidebook

The Feast: A Parable of the Ring

Marketing Your Book on a Budget

## Susan Cramer Mystery's

Scrambled

Sunny Side-Up

# A RIVER OF STONES

## KATHRYN ELIZABETH JONES

Idea Creations Press

www.ideacreationspress.com

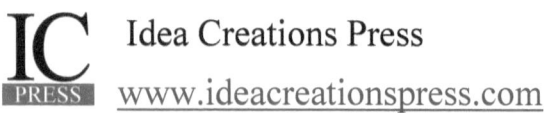

Idea Creations Press

www.ideacreationspress.com

ISBN-13: 978-0988810761

ISBN-10: 098881076X

Printed in the U.S.A.

# Dedication

To Bethany, my youngest daughter and first reader, thank you for your love and encouragement. And to my parents and husband, my love to you.

# Preface

I hope you see reflected in this book the heartfelt emotions of a child. Samantha is a witness, as we all are, to change. She sees the divorce of her parents as only a child can see it—with eyes wide open and a heart waiting to be loved no matter what.

.

# PROLOGUE

I was eight when it happened. The year was 1968 and it was morning. My mother sat my brother, Luke, and me down on the worn green couch and stared at us.

Luke nudged me. I nudged back. He nudged me again before Mother forced us to quit by sitting between us.

My mother looked at us, teary eyed, like we'd done something wrong. "Your father left last night."

"Where did he go?" I asked, unaware that he was gone for good—that he would never tuck me in bed again, or eat dinner with us, or just sit next to me on the living room couch as we watched TV.

"He is living somewhere else."

Luke broke into tears. "I want Daddy!"

How could he leave? Didn't he love us anymore?

My mother had huge globs of tears in her deep brown eyes. Her thick hair was wadded in a messy bun, and her small hands shook against the orange and red flowered robe she always wore around the house when she wasn't going anywhere.

"It's just us now," she said.

What did she mean, "just us"? Daddy hadn't died. He would still come over, wouldn't he? We would visit him, wouldn't we?

All I could do was sit there on the old green couch as Mother told us about the divorce, my mind going crazy with confusion. Why would Daddy leave us? Could someone just decide one day not to love you anymore?

Mother's divorce was final a year later. I missed Daddy, but I tried to keep myself busy with other things so I wouldn't have to think about him. I had two close friends, one who lived a few blocks away and one down about six houses—a cute boy. No, no one knew about my secret love, not even my best girlfriend, June; she always told people what I said. And because I didn't want my words to come back every which way but right, I didn't share the feelings I had for Bruce.

Bruce didn't seem to like girls. He was my age, but I had heard somewhere that boys didn't grow or mature until long after girls did. I didn't know then that maturity meant more than growing taller, or your body filling out; it meant the stuff inside, too—and I'm not just talking about the guts.

Mother and Daddy had never taken me to church, but Mother had taught me about God. She believed that God didn't belong in church with all the fake people, but that he visited those who were humble before him.

And so, every night I wished that when I woke up my body would be taller and more mature. It was the only way I could see to help Mother. Her eyes were lonely and often I would see her looking somewhere far away. I knew I could take away some of her sadness if only I were old enough to work.

I knew that Daddy's work had provided food for us, and a roof over our heads and even clothes on our backs, but until he was gone, I had no idea how much I'd taken those basic needs for granted.

In the morning, I would cry just a little and go into the kitchen for breakfast. Sometimes we'd get Cheerios without milk, or bread with a little butter, but I tried not to complain. Mother was having a hard enough time.

Six months following the divorce, Mother introduced Luke and me to her "new friend." His name was Carl. Mother started to smile again, and we got more food in the house. But I was confused. I missed my real daddy and I didn't think replacing him was going to work even if it made Mother happy.

Two months later, Mother and Carl married. It was a small wedding. Mother wore a pink dress with a thick, shiny hair ribbon around her waist. She looked beautiful, but I couldn't help feeling alone.

Carl lived with us after that, and my feelings of security returned—almost like before. Carl tried to be my daddy. He'd help me with homework and we would play games of checkers until Luke got jealous, but usually my thoughts would return to my real daddy and how much I loved and missed him.

Almost a year after Mom introduced us to Carl he adopted us. I will never forget the day we went before the judge, who sat behind his huge, wood desk, much bigger and grander than any they allowed you to sit at during school. His face was as old as a gnarled tree, and his voice sounded like God's.

He asked, "Do you children understand what you are doing?"

My brother and I nodded yes. Luke was eight and I was almost ten. I wondered if Luke really knew what he was doing, but more importantly, I wondered if I knew what I was doing and if my mother knew what she was doing.

My mother no longer had to listen to anything my daddy said. The divorce papers had been finalized, and she had a new husband. Mother had a new man who wanted to be our daddy. He looked different than our first daddy, and talked differently and everything. He had dark hair where Daddy's was light brown. And brown eyes where Daddy's were blue. Carl was shorter and looked like he lifted weights. Daddy's body looked much like mine—with legs like beanpoles in shorts.

Of course, Daddy wasn't wearing shorts that day, but a nice suit. And he looked nice, too. I didn't have to look at his skinny legs.

He sat across from my brother and me, from Mother and her new husband. Sometimes his blue eyes would search my own, but I couldn't tell what he was saying. Did he like that he was giving my brother and me away? Did it bother him that Carl was adopting us?

Don't ask me why, but I wanted it to happen. It had been so strange not having a daddy in the house. And Carl was nice. Mother smiled almost all of the time now. And I wanted Mother to smile most of all.

In the end, I wasn't sure why Mother looked so sad, but the judge shook our hands and I gave my old daddy a hug. I don't remember if he cried, because suddenly Carl's hand was reaching out. I took it. We walked arm in arm to the station wagon and got in. That was the last time I saw or heard from my daddy for a long time.

* * *

I think it was the letter that did it, the awful letter that was written after Daddy and Mother divorced. You know how sometimes you forget things, and then at the most terrible times you remember them?

"Why doesn't Daddy come to get us anymore?" I remember asking Mother.

I was crying those great big sobs that make your bones rattle and your teeth chatter, and Mommy was trying to comfort me.

"You wrote the letter, remember? A few months after the divorce?"

Yes, the letter. What had I said? Had I been so cruel that he wouldn't even call me on the telephone?

I tried to pull the words I'd written from my brain, but I couldn't remember any of it. My mother helped me out. She reminded me that I had told my father that I had a new daddy and that it was just too confusing to have two. She said that he must love me very much to respect my decision.

I wish I hadn't written those awful words. He hated me for sure now. I just knew he would never talk to me again.

I went to my bedroom and opened my dresser drawer where I kept the red bikini top with the ruffles. Pulling off my yellow shirt with the daisy embroidered on it, I pulled it on.

My mother hated that top. She hated it because Daddy had bought it, and because it showed my belly, but mostly because Daddy had bought it.

I went outside, found my pink Sting-Ray bike, climbed onto it, and rode away. My wheels made a clip-clop sound as they pummeled the Crazy Eight card I had clipped to the thin wire spokes.

I didn't stop at Bruce's, either. I rode past the house with the wicked Doberman dog and turned the corner heading toward the school. I didn't care that Mother had warned me not to go to the school late at night. It was eight o'clock and time for bed, but I just didn't care.

I went to the schoolyard and sat there in a daze, my bike leaning against the fence. Then I was in a swing, soaring as high as I could. The wind was still hot but it cooled my face like a huge fan in the giant sky. I breathed in the scent of pine and rose and closed my eyes, trying to shut out the noise of children and their parents.

But it was no use. In only seconds, the swing began to jerk, to hop in the air like a great firecracker. Still, I didn't stop my flight. If my neck jerked free, my head would go sailing through the air and I'd never have to go home again.

# CHAPTER 1

My mother didn't believe in spanking her children, but being punished by having to stay inside during nice weather seemed just as bad. I hadn't come home on time; so what? It was like I'd committed a horrible crime or something.

Luke grinned at me while I mashed my face against the living room window, watching him play outside without me. It was cars today.

Large tablespoons from the kitchen drawer had been smuggled outside and into the dirt. Tunnels had been dug. Garages had been made without me. Life was moving forward and I was stuck, punished, inside the house.

Even though my mother was continually asking about the tablespoons, about bringing them back into the house, we never did. It was as though an evil ground monster had taken them underneath the earth, never again to be discovered. We'd forget them at first, and then later we'd go outside at our mother's request to find them. They could never be found, kind of like the book called *The Borrowers*, where all these little people, about the size of your finger, steal stuff, like spools of thread, that they never return.

\* \* \*

Bruce smiled. "So she decided to let you out," he said, pulling my braided ponytail. I was wearing the red top without the middle that Mother hated. After one day of being punished, Mother said I was driving her crazy, even though all I was trying to do was to talk to her about Daddy. Bruce and I were standing in the front yard and I was getting all goose pimply just thinking about him.

"Want to come to my house?" he asked.

"Sure," I said, not really wanting to, but wanting to at the same time.

Bruce had a long scar on the side of his neck, kind of like bacon in a frying pan. It weirded me out.

One day in the heat of summer, my next-door neighbor, Steven String, had snuck a box of matches from his mother's pantry and brought them down to Bruce's house. He and Bruce lit one match and then another, letting the flames travel up the stick. When the flames reached their fingers, they blew the match out and tossed the remaining stick to the ground and lit another. Only the last time when Bruce lit his match and tried to blow it out, it caught fire to his blond hair and whisked up his neck like a roadrunner racing up a racetrack. After that, it attacked the lawn. Half of the grass was burned to ash before his daddy was able to smother the flames with water.

"We haven't put in the new lawn yet," Bruce said, knowing that would make a big difference to me. "Wanna play cars?"

I nodded. I could never get enough soil. It squished deliciously between my fingers and grew warm and pliable within the hollows of my hand.

We walked to his backyard.

"Wow!" I said, surveying the hilly land.

"My dad is fixing up the yard before he plants the grass."

"Cool!" I said, taking a metal spoon from his hand. "Maybe we can make a cave and go inside! Where did he get all the dirt anyway?"

Bruce pointed at the back of his house. "We have a basement now," he said.

I walked over to look at the area. Sure enough, there was an empty space with furniture inside. "Why didn't you come down and get me so that I could help?" I asked.

Thoughts of digging such an incredible hole excited me. And yet, Bruce hadn't called me for some reason. I knelt down on the cool soil.

"Only grown-ups could help," he said.

"Men, I suppose," I answered, craning my neck around to look at him for a moment before plunging the spoon into the newly turned soil. I knew men were stronger than women, but when Daddy was living with us, Mother was always complaining that he would forget to take out the garbage or fix the fence or bring the milk home from the supermarket on his way home from work. It was like Daddy never did anything and she did everything. I wondered if Daddy would have forgotten to come over if he'd been asked, and if Mother would have come over to help in his place. Even so, I also knew other men weren't at all like my daddy and never would be.

Bruce knelt in front of me. Like a bulldozer, he scooped up big handfuls of earth, throwing the dirt over his shoulder. "Yep," he answered. "Only men are strong enough for dirt lifting and digging out basements."

I nodded, suddenly thinking of Daddy all alone in his one-room apartment, doing nothing. And then, just as suddenly, I was thinking of Mother.

She was happy now, as happy as I'd ever seen her. So what was wrong with me?

When I was doing nothing, all I would think about was Daddy. And when I was with someone else that was practically all I thought about too, except for Bruce, of course. He was the only happiness in my entire life.

# CHAPTER 2

I wasn't invited to the wedding. I know this because I overheard Mother and Carl speaking about Daddy's wedding from behind the closed door in their bedroom. Evidently, they hadn't been invited either.

"He wants to begin a new life…" was all I needed to hear to convince me that I had lost my daddy for good. That day, I stopped roller-skating.

By the time I was ten, I'd grown out of the red bikini top with the fluffy front and traded in my skimpy outfit for a pair of flare jeans.

I was practically a teenager now, and knew it.

School was not as important as my social life. I was in desperate need of a female friend—any female who would take me in and love me, no matter what, would be fine with me.

Perhaps that's why I started hanging out with June. She was different from anyone else I knew. She accepted me from day one. She didn't care that my parents had divorced but felt desperately sorry that my mother was happier than I was.

"Samantha, let me hypnotize you," she said one day in the heat of summer.

We were in her father's trailer. I didn't like her father. He was like most grown-ups who talked and forgot to listen. His wife had left him a year ago but I didn't care; he hated us playing inside his trailer.

"You don't really want to hypnotize me," I answered, rolling my eyes at her. "Do you think it will actually work?"

"Of course!" she said proudly. "Now sit here." She directed me to the floral cushion near the west window.

I sat.

"Now close your eyes."

I giggled.

"Be quiet!"

"What about putting me to sleep with an old stopwatch?"

"That stuff never works. The newer guys always have you close your eyes."

I closed my eyes to the sound of her somber voice. "You will sleep now…sleep…sleep…" June went on for a few minutes about how I would be very sleepy.

I tried not to laugh. And for one strange moment I almost felt trancelike as I thought about how sleepy I'd become. And then suddenly June said, "Open your eyes!"

My blue eyes flicked open.

"Now…I want you to go to my dad and kiss him on the cheek…"

"Right…now?" I asked.

"Yes, right now. You will do everything I say…you are hypnotized!"

Well, two things were for sure. First, I was not hypnotized, and second, I was not going inside the house to kiss her father. But I tried to remain calm and act hypnotized.

"OK…" I stood, flicked the latch to the camper door, and walked, zombie-like, to the back door of her house.

Halfway there I stopped. "Where am I?" I asked, turning myself about like some wind-up clock.

"You are on your way…to my dad," she said in a somber whisper that wasn't quite a whisper, pushing me slightly on the back to move me forward.

"No…I am not," I countered, turning to face her. "I am no longer…hypnotized."

June waved her hand in front of my eyes. In that moment her red hair seemed even more vibrant and the dots of her freckles seemed to connect.

"I did it! I did it!" she screamed, jumping up and down in front of me. "I can hardly believe it. With a little more practice I'll have you eating out of my hand."

I smiled. "Let's play King of Bunker Hill," I said.

* * *

18

"Ouch!"

Mother leaned over me. "Does this hurt?" she asked, wiggling the pinky on my right hand.

"Ouch!" I wailed again, pulling away. "Do you think it's broken?"

"Probably not. Let's watch it for a few days and see what happens."

I nodded. I didn't want to go to the doctor and I was glad she wasn't going to make me. It was bad enough that I had lost at Bunker Hill. Half a dozen times I had tried to push June from the hill, fighting to be on top. But June was obviously stronger than I was and so in the end she had won, breaking my finger in the process.

June only laughed when she saw me a couple of days later. "I think it really is broken," she said. She stared at the swollen joint, grossly fascinated. "Has Bruce seen it?"

I didn't answer her. I flinched, pulling back. Well, it was broken all right. I wondered how long it would hurt. A few more days? Or would it last for weeks?

When the swelling went down, I noticed that my finger had healed bent slightly to the right. The crooked joint held a special kind of awe for spectators after that. I would put a mouth and eyes on the tip of my pinky's flesh and pretend the thing was speaking with a broken neck.

* * *

My next-door neighbor, Mr. String, was an animal killer. I always found that strange: cats love string but Mr. String hated cats. Mr. String had a wife and two kids—a boy named Steven (who had helped to catch Bruce's neck on fire) and a girl about three years old, named Candy.

Although Steven and Candy and I spent a lot of time together, making tunnels in the ground, playing war, and getting married, I never thought for one moment that Mr. String would kill our cat.

Our cat's name was Tiger, because he had golden stripes just like the real kind. Mother would always make us get male cats because female cats produced babies. Sometimes, however, the mother cat

19

would come to live at our house with the father cat and then everything would be grand.

And everything might have been grand if our neighbor hadn't poisoned our cat. Days can be pretty terrible when you lose your best cat.

"If you don't keep that cat out of my yard, I'm going to kill him!" Mr. String had screamed at me more than once.

And that's exactly what happened.

I came outside to dig in the dirt with my famous spoon one day, only to find Tiger underneath the bushes nearby. He was as straight and still as if he'd been in the freezer for ten years. His eyes were open and bulging, staring wide in fright.

I bent near him, touching his silky fur, and froze. He was dead. My neighbor had killed him and I would never forgive him.

* * *

Bruce, who was still my secret love, was making fun of me. "Why won't you kiss me?" he asked as we sat huddled underneath the plastic swimming pool in my backyard, which served as our secret fort. Maybe June's hypnotic suggestions had played havoc with my brain. I wouldn't kiss her daddy; no, I couldn't do that. Someone else, however, could most assuredly kiss me. Perhaps there was something to this hypnotism after all.

I would be entering my fifth year of elementary school in the fall. But it was summer now, and the breeze wafted above us like an invisible fan. I had dreamt of this moment since I was seven. And now it was here! Bruce's words shot at me like a lightening bolt, sending an excited chill down my spine. Like King of Bunker Hill, I was totally unprepared. But I wanted more than anything to take the leap of faith and kiss him.

And so, I did.

The kiss was quick, more like a bird's peck and not like those beautifully romantic highlights in every movie I had seen with kissing in it—bodies and lips pressed together like a grand peanut butter sandwich. But the warmth that caressed my spine was unmistakable. My heart floated within me, and my eyes closed as I reveled in what had just happened.

And then, quite suddenly, the pool was pushed over and Bruce was gone, leaving me alone to ponder the moment without him.

"Bruce, stop!" I yelled from the pit. But he was long gone.

I brushed the dirt off my shorts and ran after him. "Bruce! Bruce! Wait!"

When I found him he was in his backyard, huddled behind the tool shed. His breath was coming loose in heated gasps. He wouldn't look at me.

Well, it was just as well. I was so embarrassed I could hardly stand it. I sat down next to him, breathing in the smell of his hair and the dirt. Oh, how I loved him! But he was so still. He might have been dead if I hadn't known otherwise.

A few moments later he turned to me. "That was weird," he said.

"Yeah," I answered, "weird." I hid my glow of pleasure.

"Sam, don't tell anyone, OK?" he asked. Bruce dug his heel in the dirt, rubbing it back and forth and making a trail with his shoe.

"OK," I answered. I wouldn't even tell June! How could I?

"Promise?"

"Promise."

Bruce stood. "I've got to go in now," he said, shoving his hands into his back pockets.

"OK. Want to play tomorrow?"

"Maybe." Bruce was at the back door. "Remember, don't tell."

I nodded, totally embarrassed and truly and utterly unsure of how I was supposed to keep this secret. I wasn't even sure I wanted to. I didn't like secrets. There were too many of them flying around in my house already. Secrets my mother held behind her eyes that she wouldn't share with me. Secrets spoken behind closed doors that Mother didn't want me to know about. Even a distance between my brother and me that I couldn't understand. It was like I was living in someone else's house and playacting like I liked it. But I would try.

# CHAPTER 3

June was laughing. "He did what?" She smirked.

"Kissed me," I answered. "But you can't say anything."

I'd waited two weeks to tell her. For two weeks I'd thought about the situation. Would she respect my wishes this time? Or would she blurt out what I'd said, like every other time?

Actually, I was having a difficult time holding my feelings in. I couldn't tell my mother or my brother, but I had to tell someone. My mother wouldn't have understood and Luke would have laughed at me like I was stupid.

But June seemed impressed. "Well, it was only a matter of time," she said, sounding more like a soap opera than herself. "He looks over at you, you know, when you think he isn't looking."

"Really?"

June nodded, the secret of a lifetime now unfolded. "I guess I should have told you sooner. I hypnotized him once…"

"Who…Bruce?"

"Yep. Right there in the trailer." She giggled.

"You're lying," I said. Actually I thought June might be telling the truth, and that worried me.

"He told me how much he liked you."

"Really?" I was repeating myself like crazy but I just couldn't help it. "What else did he say?"

"Oh, I don't know. I don't remember anything else."

"Did he tell you that he was going to kiss me?"

"I don't think so. I think I would remember that. But, yes, I do remember something."

"What?"

"How blue his eyes were. Did you know how blue his eyes get when he's hypnotized?"

"No, how?"

"Like that lake we went to last summer. Remember the lake?"

"I remember." Bear Lake was perhaps my favorite spot to think, other than the swing at the school ground. The water there was a deep, crisp blue, and as calm as the sun just before rising.

"Well, he was looking at me and I could have sworn he was going to kiss me," June was saying.

"What?" The blue lake of my mind filled with mud and the waters heaved off the bank.

"Just kidding." June laughed, but I didn't echo her laugh. I thought about how stupid I felt.

* * *

Bruce wouldn't look at me, and school was difficult enough without him refusing to look at me. June had obviously talked to him about the kiss.

Because of Bruce, and June's words to him, I was having a hard time keeping up with my work; actually I didn't want to do it at all. I couldn't concentrate. My mind had flown away to another country or something.

Add to that what I'd heard two nights before, behind my mother's closed door, and, well, let me just say that it was worse than anything I'd heard since my daddy left us. It was even worse than June telling Bruce she knew about our kiss. It was the kind of news that made you wonder why you'd even been born. And I don't know if I can even tell you what my mother said except I promised myself that I would tell you the complete truth, so here it is.

"I hate you!" I screamed. "Why didn't you tell me I had a stepbrother?" I stood behind the closed door, my heart pounding, my eyes flaming. I could almost smell the scent of my tennis shoes burning on the green-carpeted floor, my breath heaving open the door. Another lie. How could they do this to me? Secrets, secrets, secrets. How many secrets were there?

Carl opened the bedroom door so quickly a breeze flew into my eyes and made me cough. But the fire within me didn't blow out. My mother got up from the bed, her brown eyes bugged out like those of my dead cat, and Carl only looked at me with a straight smile. Luke was in the hall by then and walking over to Carl. "Do you really mean I have a brother?" he asked.

Carl smiled and placed his thick arm around Luke's shoulders. "Yes, you have a brother."

"What's his name?"

"Joshua."

"How old is he?" Luke was standing so close to Carl they looked like Siamese twins.

"About your age, near ten."

"I can't believe it! Would he be in my class at school?"

"I don't see why not. I've already talked to Mrs. Granger."

I thought I'd spit. I'd seen many boys do it on the street but doubted that I'd get away with it, even now. Still, I felt like doing it. Had I known that Carl had a son I would never have allowed him to adopt me. The question from the judge rang in my ears. "Do you two know what you are doing?"

No. No. No. It was like the skeleton that some people say lives in closets had walked out of my mother's closet and chopped half of my body off.

Yes, I knew Carl had had a wife before my mother. I'd never seen her, just like I'd never seen my father's new wife. But one night I'd overheard Carl talking about her to my mother when he thought no one was listening. He didn't seem to like her much, and complained about all her faults like they were droppings her dog had left.

Not only did she have a dog that crapped all over the lawn, but she also owned a seventeen-year-old cat named Musty that had finally died of old age. I figured the cat must have had some sort of smelly fur or that I'd mistaken the name Misty for Musty.

Anyway, I knew I would hate Joshua. For one thing, I would have to treat him like a brother even though he was a stranger. Not that I treated Luke that good, but in the back of my mind I could remember the closeness we'd shared before the divorce. Would I have to kiss up to Joshua and make him feel at home and do every other stupid thing my mother wanted me to do? Would I have to wash the dishes while he dried them? Sit at the table with him and look over at his stupid face? Wash my mother's car with him breathing at me from the other side of the window? Well, even if I had to do all those things and more, one thing was for sure: I would never like him, and that was that.

"I can't believe you didn't tell me!" I screamed.

Everyone was standing around gaping at me. But I didn't care.

"I don't see my daddy anymore! This…this man comes into our house and pretends like he's my daddy! And now, now I have another brother? I hate you all!"

I thought my head would pop off, but I kept screaming the hateful words until I couldn't scream any more.

# CHAPTER 4

Joshua was fat—so fat that I thought I'd spill over laughing when I saw him. His cheeks looked like pale rubber tires, and when his mouth grinned, his orange freckles blended in with the rest of his stupid face.

Carl wasn't fat, so I figured it must have been the woman he'd been married to before Mother who made Joshua that way. Joshua stood before me in the living room, along with my mother and his father, Carl. Carl motioned to me with his eyes. Luke couldn't seem to speak.

"Follow me," I said, leading Joshua down the hallway to his new room.

Joshua followed. I could feel his heavy breath on my neck as he *chug-chugged* his way behind me.

"Mother put you in the office room," I said, stopping for a moment and looking over at his wide brown eyes. "Before you came she painted it blue with a giant fish on the wall. I think it's a whale," I said, hardly believing I was telling him these things.

"Thanks, Sam," he grunted.

"No problem," I answered. "Here it is."

I wasn't sure why my mother had suggested I take him to his room. It was as if I were the doorman or something.

"So, where's your room?" he asked, filling the doorway.

"Down the hall by Mother's," I said.

"Oh," he answered, blundering into the room. He sat his large suitcase with the brown flap on the floor and plunked himself on the bed, making the springs squeak.

\* \* \*

Luke was quiet for a change. Sometimes he yapped so much I could hardly stand it. Perhaps he was part dog. I couldn't see Joshua anywhere. Luke sat on the lawn, seemingly waiting for my return. It was Saturday. I'd spent the day at June's even though I was being punished for mouthing off at Carl. But grounding at my house never lasted for too long. I even wondered if my mother had already forgotten about it.

"Where is the ten-year-old disaster?" I asked, transferring my heavy books to my left hip.

"You mean Josh? With Dad, of course."

"Carl," I corrected.

Luke breathed heavily. "The viewing. The funeral for Joshua's mother is tomorrow, remember?"

"Did Mother go?"

"Of course she went. Potpies are in the freezer. You're going to be skinned alive when she gets back."

I tried to ignore Luke's comment. So what if I got grounded for a week more?

"How long will they be gone?" I asked, pretty sure I never wanted them to come home again.

"Dad didn't say, and Mother rushed out without even telling me good-bye. Why are you crying?"

"I'm not."

"Your eyes are wetting themselves then, " he said, standing to wipe my cheek with his grungy hand.

"Don't," I said, looking away from him. "I mean it."

We were silent for a moment, looking at nothing. Finally Luke said, "Sam, having a new brother isn't so bad, you know." He brushed his heavy brown hair from his eyes.

"That's because you're a boy," I answered, sniffing.

Luke seemed to take in my thoughts. He adjusted his feet from underneath his seat to sprawling out in front. "Josh seems nice enough."

"For a whale," I answered, mussing Luke's hair.

Luke didn't look at me. "I've waited a long time for a brother," he finally said, looking me in the eyes and brushing his hair down. "You're great, for a sister, so don't feel bad." He smiled over at me as if in the smile he could somehow make me feel better. "I still love you, Sis."

But I didn't believe him. I couldn't stand the fact that Luke cared more about Joshua now than he did about me. Sometimes I would listen at Joshua's bedroom door and hear them talking about guy stuff—trucks and snakes and fishing with your bare hands. Luke had obviously tricked Joshua into thinking you could find loads of fish at Bear Lake. I didn't understand how I was somehow less important to him than his new brother just because I was a girl, and part of me said I didn't care.

Still, I wondered what was so terribly wrong with me. I wasn't a boy, but so what? Before the divorce I'd seemed good enough. Luke and I had talked, sharing our feelings about school and friends and stuff. So why was I no longer good enough for him?

* * *

June and I sat on our individual swings as I spilled my guts. It was after nine o'clock and my mother was still gone. "I must be going crazy," I said, brushing my feet against the half-moon soil beneath me.

"I had an aunt who went crazy," she said.

I looked at her in surprise, my right hand unclasped from the link of chain.

"I'm not kidding, Sam. They found her in her bedroom. All of the knifes from the kitchen drawer were piled on top of her bed. With one of them, she'd slit her wrists."

I gulped. No, I guess I wasn't that crazy. "No, I mean, with the divorce..."

"You're still hurting, huh?" June asked.

"I guess so," I answered.

"Maybe it will take a few more months. When my mother left two years ago, it took my dad almost a year before he started dating anyone else." She laughed as if the comment seemed funny.

I didn't know what to say. Instead I planted my feet firmly on the ground and pushed off. In only moments I was swinging in the October air. June joined me.

A few minutes later she stopped and asked me to do the same. Dragging my long legs on the ground once, then twice as the swing came to a halt, I looked eagerly into her face. "What?" I asked.

"Want me to hypnotize you?"

"Why?"

"Because. Here. Close your eyes." June jumped off her swing and stood before me like a grand statue in the wrong place. For surely this was the wrong place and I was the wrong person. Still, in the deepest part of my soul I knew I couldn't do this thing alone.

"You are getting sleepy...the divorce doesn't bother you at all...in fact, you are quite happy with it...your new brother doesn't bother you either...you decide you like him. You are a happy person..."

I kept my eyes closed the whole time, listening to her soothing words that held nothing but lies, especially the part about being happy. And when June was finished, I thanked her.

# CHAPTER 5

"So, what are you supposed to be?" I asked June. She and I were walking to school with Bruce.

June was dressed entirely in black. A thick band of material of the same color was wrapped around her red hair and forehead. Her thin waist was cinched tightly by a red belt, and she wore matching shoes that were much too large for her.

"A karate instructor," Bruce said, bowing as was the custom.

I laughed. June frowned.

"I'm a hypnotist, of course. Don't I look like one?"

"Nope," Bruce drawled, getting into the farmer talk of his character.

Bruce was dressed as a farmer, and he really looked like one too. His mother had sewn uneven patches of old plaid material on the knees of his jeans, and Bruce wore an old straw hat and fake whiskers on his chin, probably painted with his mother's eye pencil.

June seemed momentarily offended. "What do you know, anyway?" She looked over at me. "You're probably the only person in the entire school not dressed up."

Well, she was partly right. About half the school was dressed up in some kind of Halloween attire. But it just wasn't the same as in kindergarten.

I had been a ballerina that year and everyone, including Luke, thought I was beautiful. I could see it in his eyes. I felt beautiful too, mainly because I'd been dancing for almost a year and thought I was a professional, like the figure skaters in the Olympics. At every house the lady would say, "Oh, how cute!" or something equally positive. I arrived home with invisible wings. It was as if I could have flown everywhere without ever having to land on the ground again.

* * *

"Trick or treat!" The little girl's muffled voice on the other side of the door made me dream of the past, but just for a moment.

"Aren't you going to answer the door?" Mother asked. She was in the kitchen with me. In the other room the television blared something about vampires seeking out their prey down lonely streets.

"Sure, Mom." I opened the door to give out the candy bars I held within the orange bucket. June's face stared back at me and made me jump.

"Surprised you, didn't I?" she asked. She was wearing the same costume she had worn at school and still looked like a karate instructor.

"Yeah," I answered.

She laughed. "I've brought someone with me."

Out stepped Bruce, with the same sort of attire, only he was wearing a black belt instead of a red one. I almost laughed. A black belt. And then, to my surprise, my mother said, "I already have your outfit ready."

"What?"

I turned to see her holding a black pair of pants, a black shirt from Carl's closet, a green tie and a braided belt—the new one I'd just purchased for school.

"A hippie?" I asked.

June frowned. "No, silly. A hypnotist like us!"

Mother smiled. "I thought you'd want to go," she said, giving me a quick side hug and brushing my long hair with her fingers. For a moment my mind was transported to the past. We were standing in the bathroom, and Daddy was watching us from the doorway as Mother brushed my hair and pulled my two ponytails into braids.

"You want two, right?" she was asking me.

I was nodding my head and watching Daddy smiling at me. "My pretty little girl," he was saying.

I put on the strange outfit and joined my friends outside. Perhaps I'd only thought I was too old for trick-or-treating. Perhaps I'd been wrong about a lot of things.

* * *

The air was cool as we did our trick-or-treating, but at least it wasn't snowing like last year. We began at Bruce's house. His mother was giving away huge Butterfinger bars. She plunked the candy in my pillowcase and said, "Karate instructors, huh?"

I laughed. June didn't. Bruce reached inside and punched his mother lovingly on the arm. "You know what we are!" he said.

His mother laughed. "Oh, yes, I remember now." She grinned at us and sent us away.

The Doberman man and his dogs lived next door to Bruce. I'd never trick-or-treated there, mainly because of his scary dog, but also because I had never met the old man who'd moved inside a couple of years ago. This year, a never-before-seen scarecrow sat out front so we decided to stop and take a look.

"Wow!" Bruce said, looking through the holes in the chain-link fence. "Doesn't he look…real?"

The life-sized scarecrow was sitting in a metal chair. The porch light lit up his wrinkly form. He wore a brown and orange plaid shirt with lots of straw sticking out, and a pair of jeans with holes in the knees and even more straw sticking through. He had on an old farmer's hat that looked as if the Doberman had eaten half of it, and his face was wrinkled and reminded me of a mushy apple.

"Where do you think Mr. Green got it?" June asked.

I wondered how June knew the old man's name. He'd never, ever, said a word to me. But I didn't ask her.

"He probably made it," Bruce whispered.

A slight chill, one that was definitely more than the coolness of the night, crept up my back. "That thing looks…alive."

"No…he doesn't," June stuttered, tripping backward from the fence. I looked behind me and saw June ducking behind a large bush.

"Maybe Mr. Green is an artist or something." Bruce was still near the fence, and I wondered if he was just as frightened as I was.

"Maybe we should go." Bruce touched my hand for one brief second.

I jumped, but not because Bruce had touched me. "Look!" I whispered in Bruce's ear, "the scarecrow is moving its hand!"

Bruce looked through the tough wire. Very slowly, he backed away from the fence.

"Where are you going?" I grabbed at his shoulder.

"Let's go!" he whispered.

I turned. For one brief second I thought to join him. And then, as if all time stood still except for one ominous creature, the scarecrow stood and began to walk toward me.

June screamed, "Ahhh!" from behind the heavy bush, and Bruce raced away, I figured to where June was hiding. But I didn't look back. I didn't dare look back!

"Don't move!" the scarecrow yelled.

My feet were frozen. They wouldn't move. As the scarecrow walked slowly toward me, sliding its straw-infested feet in my direction, my heart jumped in fear. Still, I couldn't move. Why couldn't I move?

Two steps in front of me I could see the creature's face. It was terribly old and very hideous. I could see small veins popping from its forehead, and its lips were sort of a purple red. And then, without warning, it reached forth its arm.

I screamed. The living scarecrow laughed. "Now, you big kids aren't afraid of me, are you?"

It could speak!

The Doberman pounced from directly behind the scarecrow. The beast jumped up, reaching his front claws to the top of the fence. "Charlie! Stop!" the scarecrow yelled, and the dog cowered behind his legs, shamefaced.

The scarecrow let go of my arm and, with a sweep of its hand, took off the straw-filled hat and smudged a little of the paint off its nose.

This was probably the old man that lived here, I thought wildly to myself. Charlie? His beast's name was Charlie? I could hardly believe it.

"Mr. Green?" Bruce asked.

He bowed. "Of course."

I smiled wearily, wiping my left hand with the piece of green tie that was wrapped around my head. A few moments later, probably because she realized I wasn't going to die, June came back to the fence.

"You kids never come to the door," he said. "So this year…" he pointed to the chair sitting by the front door, "I thought I'd come to you."

"Well, you did that, Mr. Green," Bruce said. "June here, she was real scared."

The man chuckled. "Sorry about my dog," he said. "You're the boy Bruce that lives next door, aren't you? And you—aren't you that little snippet that lives up the street? Samantha, I was sorry to hear about your parents' divorce." He hesitated for only a moment. "And you, the little red-haired gal—June, is it?"

He gave her a quick wink and June nodded, placing her hands firmly in her pants pockets.

"A fine name."

For the first time in history I realized I had never seen Mr. Green close up. In fact, the only other time I'd seen him, other than tonight, was from his front window. Boy, he sure was old. This close up, his wrinkles looked like deep ruts. But his blue eyes seemed warm as he reached his hand over the fence and dropped something round in each of our pillow cases. "Caramel corn," he said, returning to his post and sitting down. And then he was as still as death as we walked away.

"Strange," I remarked as we rounded the corner in the direction of the school. "Have you ever seen Mr. Green that close up before?"

"I have," Bruce replied, placing his hand on my shoulder as we walked.

"Mr. Green. I didn't know his last name was Green," I said.

"Why not?" Bruce was looking over at me kind of funny. "I found out last winter." He removed his left hand from my shoulder. Slight chills raced up my back—chills that I tried to ignore. "You remember. Mr. Green's wife died."

"He had a wife?" June asked.

"Well, yeah. Duh, you guys." He walked in front of us to the next house. "Didn't you come to the funeral?"

"No," we answered in unison.

"But you did?" I asked, sure that Bruce would tell us the strange goings on. The creepy way the body looked, like a stiff board with a face as pale as white paint. But he was silent.

"Hurry up!"

I hurried; June followed behind me. I don't know if it was the scare of Mr. Green or the news of his dead wife that frightened me the most. Hopefully, I can—and without too much difficulty—share with you what happened next.

# CHAPTER 6

We'd covered half the neighborhood, nearly forty houses, when Bruce dared us to go trick-or-treating at the house on the hill. I was hesitant. The man who lived there was even creepier than Mr. Green. I'd never seen him, but every kid in the neighborhood knew he was a demon of some sort—maybe even a vampire. He never came out during the day, and spent his evenings in a darkened house with only a candle flickering in the window. Tonight, not even the porch light was on. There was no pumpkin in the window or on the top cement step, and nothing that would encourage anyone to come to the door. But a dare was a dare.

It also looked like the old man hadn't been out in some time to prune his hedges or pick up the miscellaneous trash left by passersby who used the sidewalk as a trash can. At the door, I couldn't see a doorbell, only a large doorknocker with a golden lion growling at me. It was like I was suddenly whisked back into the play *A Christmas Carol*, and old Scrooge was just waiting for me beyond the door.

"Let's go!" I whispered to Bruce. June was right behind me, hanging onto my leather belt.

"Chicken!" Bruce's voice rang out, and then he was silent. "Someone is moving around in there," he whispered.

Well, of course someone was, but it was the way Bruce said it, all creepy, like any minute there was going to be trouble. "Follow me," Bruce said, leading the two of us down the hill and to the cement stairs at the back of the house. "I think I heard him clomping down the stairs."

We crept on tiptoe as if the dried lawn would give us away. It made small crackling sounds but nothing more. At the top basement step Bruce yelled, "Ouch!"

"Shhhh!" June hissed.

"I kicked something," Bruce said.

I looked down at the aged steps below me. They were chipping and peeling with age. At the bottom there was a tiny window in the door, much bigger than a peephole, but higher than we could reach.

We walked down the crackling steps, passing the old potted plant that Bruce had obviously kicked with his foot. Bruce knocked. We waited. There was a small breeze that night, and the trees behind us whispered of the moaning spirits of the dead. I couldn't believe we were actually doing this. My heart thundered and my legs felt weak. I prayed silently to myself that I wouldn't pass out.

After a few moments the window went dark.

"Why did he do that?" I asked, jumping in the dark as if someone had touched me.

"I don't know," Bruce said. "Try lifting me up. I want to peek in the window."

"Maybe we should go to the Strings' house." I didn't like the feeling that was suddenly creeping through my bones.

"We'll do that last," Bruce answered. "Lift me up."

"Let me look. I'm the lightest," June said.

"Get on, then," Bruce said. He bent down and she straddled her legs onto his shoulders.

"No! Not my hair! Hang onto my shirt!" Bruce cried.

I giggled, the creepiness seeping through my skin.

"Shhh!" June said.

"See anything?" I asked.

"It's too dark," June answered. "Wait! There's someone walking around in there!"

"In the dark?" Bruce asked.

"There's a large something on the floor with a light coming out…Oh…someone just got in! Put…me down!"

Bruce scrunched back down. June slid off his shoulders, breathing heavily. Her eyes were wide with fear as she scrambled up the steps, dragging her loaded pillowcase like a dead rat. We followed in suspense.

"What's wrong?" Bruce asked. It was hard to keep up. June was taking mammoth steps, her red hair bouncing like a rubber ball. The black sash was no longer around her head.

"Slow down!" I said, my feet feeling like they were going to fall off from all the walking we'd done. "What did you see?"

I don't even know why I asked. But I wished later that I hadn't.

June looked at me with frightened eyes—they reminded me of the people's eyes in vampire movies before the vampire flies over to the victim to bite her neck. June's lips quivered. They were the pasty white of a dead person inside her coffin.

"There is a vampire in that house," she said, grabbing Bruce's shirttail, which had come untucked from his pants. Her small hand grasped the fabric, and with tear-filled eyes she began to shake. "There is a vampire in that house, and we're never going to be safe again!"

June held Bruce's shirt tightly in her hand as she walked, Bruce stumbling beside her. Only when we'd reached her house did she let go.

"My father isn't home. I can't go in there alone."

I looked at the dark windows and agreed.

June retrieved a house key from around her neck, and with shaky hands turned the knob. For a moment we stood there, half wondering if someone was home after all, someone who didn't belong there.

Bruce led us inside. June grasped onto his shirt and I followed closely behind. It was deathly silent inside except for the ticking of the grandfather clock in the living room.

"The light," June croaked, pointing her finger to a place on the wall.

There was a scramble of feet. Bruce reached up. A short *click* followed, and then a beam of light from the kitchen lit up our heads like a UFO.

June sank into a kitchen chair. She was so limp that it seemed every muscle and bone in her body had been pulled out. A splash of tears was still flowing down her pale face, and her lips were trembling.

I looked over at Bruce. His blue eyes pierced my own but he said nothing.

Finally, when the silence only made me more afraid, I decided to speak up.

"Are you sure it was a vampire?" I asked.

I couldn't have asked a worse question. June's eyes, now red and burning from crying, stung my own. "Do you think I would lie about something like that?"

"No," I mumbled, embarrassed at myself.

"There is a vampire living in that house. A vampire, Sam!"

I nodded, sure that any more words from my lips would be taken as unbelief. A few minutes later, June stood. "Turn on all the lights," she said. "I want to go to bed."

\* \* \*

I walked home with Bruce. The silence was deathly, but neither of us seemed able to speak. Bruce took my hand, but I felt nothing but comfort. There was no room for romance tonight, only staying together so that we would be safe.

The moon was full, and I tried not to watch it or the other trick-or-treaters as Bruce walked me back to my house. The wind had died down, but in its place I heard the voices of children.

At my door, Bruce looked at me oddly and then kissed me good-bye on the cheek. I watched him walk down my sidewalk and turn the corner toward home. Only then did I go inside.

\* \* \*

Joshua and Luke came home from their own trick-or-treating an hour later. Fortunately, the vampire movie was finished by the time I got home and not blaring in the living room. I took off my costume and put on my silky blue pajamas. But I could not sleep. June's words continued to terrify me in the worst possible way.

Every time I heard a noise, I jumped. Every time I heard my mother's voice, my heart would beat quicker. I had to sleep with my back to the wall just in case something popped out from under the bed or behind the window.

My closet was shut and my window curtain as well, but I hadn't dared close my bedroom door. The hall light drifted into the otherwise dark space and gave me some comfort. I'd long since given up my night-light but I would have been happy to have it then. My skin had never crawled so much.

39

# CHAPTER 7

It was one o'clock before I had a chance to talk with Bruce. Between making my bed and doing my chores, I felt like a regular Cinderella.

I was pretty tired when I finished, and I had just shut the front door behind me when Joshua suddenly appeared, coming toward me. I stopped dead center in the middle of the lawn. "What?" I asked.

"Where ya going?"

"None of your business."

"I'm bored," he said, as if I cared.

"Where's Luke?"

"Over at Steve's."

"Why don't you join them?"

"Steve doesn't like me...and anyway, I want to hang out with you."

"Why?"

"I like you."

"Thanks," I mumbled. "But you can't come."

In that second I saw Luke stumbling around the corner of the house, his brown hair blowing in the chilly air. Steve wasn't with him. "Hey, Sis!" he said.

"Hey..." I answered, looking up the street to where Bruce was waiting for me. "Can we talk later? I gotta go."

Joshua looked over at Luke, and Luke over at Joshua. Suddenly Joshua grabbed my T-shirt and held on tight.

"We...think you should stay here," Luke said.

"Let go!"

"Not until you promise to spend some time with us."

Both Joshua and Luke looked at me intently, as if they wanted me for lunch. I wasn't about to give in. What did they really have planned?

I tried to break free of Joshua's hold, but his grip was too tight. I could smell Joshua's heavy sweat accumulating on his rubbery face. Luke reached out and grabbed the other side of my orange T-shirt. He was grinning like an evil pumpkin.

All I could think about was how much I hated them both.

"Let go!"

"Not on your life!" they said in unison, as if they'd planned this entire event. What if they had?

"I'll tell Mother. Mother! Mo—!" Joshua clamped his white hand over my mouth. It tasted just like salt.

"Mmmmmaaaa," I mumbled. I twisted my body, kicked my legs, and finally gave up, breathing like a prisoner who wanted her escape but would have to suffer a few years longer.

"Are you ready to give up?" Luke asked, scowling at me.

I nodded my head. Very slowly, Joshua released his hand from over my mouth. Spit had accumulated on his hand, and he wiped it against his Levi's. I smiled inwardly.

"We're going to play cowboys and Indians," Luke reported. "You're the squaw."

"OK," I said. "What do I do?"

Luke grinned, his large teeth glistening in the afternoon air. "Come with me," he said. "I'm the chief." He turned and strode away, Joshua sandwiching me between them.

I almost laughed. "You gonna take your shirt off?" I asked. Luke had already turned the corner and was probably getting set up for battle. "I don't know of any Indians who wear shirts."

"Good idea, squaw," he said, reaching down with his pudgy fingers. He had the blue cloth over his face when I made my escape. I heard a second of grunting and got a brief glance at Joshua's fat stomach bouncing before I burst free.

I dashed to the end of the lawn, turned the corner, and ran swiftly to the end of the street. There was no sound from my house. Evidently Joshua was still struggling to get his shirt off.

I laughed and ran to Bruce's backyard, my breath puffing like a steam train in the olden days. I stopped quickly when I saw Bruce. He was standing alone at the foot of what looked like a small bridge,

41

his blond hair blowing in the autumn breeze. My heart skipped a beat, and then I ran over to him.

The hills and valleys supported the wooden bridge, and underneath it water trickled slowly between the rocks.

"You won't believe me," Bruce said, grabbing my arm and walking me to the small twig called a tree leaning leisurely over the newly built bridge. We sat. "Take off your shoes," he said. "I won't tell."

"Tell what?"

"My mom doesn't want us to put our feet in here," he said. "I turned it on after she left," he added, pointing to the place near the house where the water valve must have been. "She's gone to have her hair done. Dad's out golfing."

I smiled. "They leave you here alone?"

"Don't need no babysitter."

I laughed. He was right. What ten-year-old needed someone to tell him what to do? Still, I hadn't wanted to be alone the entire day. Thoughts of a vampire running around at night in the neighborhood gave me the willies.

I put my feet in the water. "Ooooh!" I shrieked, pulling them back out.

Bruce looked at me strangely and then slowly placed his feet in the chilling water. I put my shoes and socks back on.

"June will be over in a minute. But I wanted to tell you first."

"June?"

"She has a right to know too."

I nodded.

"They say a Mr. Grant lives in that house."

"Who says?"

"My parents. I asked them last night before we went trick-or-treating."

"Before…?"

"Uh huh. They say he's a hermit, and that he can't go out of his house because he can't walk and something is wrong with his heart. Evidently, this guy has his food brought in to him by different family members. He comes out at night to feed and water his plants but nothing more."

"What kind of body parts?" I asked.

"What?"

"You know, for his food. Do they bring him human necks or what?"

Bruce placed his hand over his mouth. "I never thought of that," he whispered. "I was thinking they brought him regular food!"

A death chill raced up my back. "Why does he come out at night to water his plants? Why can't it be in the morning, for heaven's sake? I'll tell you why. It's because he's a vampire…"

"That part I had figured out," Bruce said. "That's why I wanted to go over there last night and see for myself."

"But you didn't see for yourself. You took us!"

I was suddenly angry and more scared than I'd ever been in my entire life.

"I'm sorry." Bruce looked down at his feet. I could see he was thinking hard about what to say next. That's when I heard June's voice behind me.

"Hey, you guys!"

I jumped as if I'd been stabbed in the neck.

Bruce waved her to the bridge. June sat, taking off her shoes without so much as an invitation. "Wow!" she said, placing her painted toenails into the water. "I couldn't sleep the entire night. I tried to hypnotize myself, but I was so nervous I couldn't get it to work."

Bruce laughed. "You would have been hypnotized forever if it had worked."

"I thought of that later," she said. "Neither of you guys know how to do it. You would have had to take me to a real hypnotist to get me to snap out of it. It doesn't matter anyway. I got so tired I just fell asleep."

I didn't dare tell them I'd had to go to sleep with the door open and the hall light on. Still, I felt some comfort knowing someone else had been as afraid as I was.

"June, I was just telling Sam about Mr. Grant," Bruce said.

"Who?"

"The vampire. My parents say he's a hermit, has people bringing meals to him, and that he only comes out at night…"

"What did you see…exactly?" I asked June again, though I wondered if she'd get as angry as the night before.

June shivered in the November air, but she didn't remove her feet from the icy water. "Well, at first it was hard to tell, kind of like a shadow that comes from your body that you can hardly believe is yours, and then it turned. All I could see was the glow of the coffin and the outline of the vampire in front of it."

"Why would a vampire's coffin be lit up?" I asked.

June shrugged her shoulders. "I don't know."

"Maybe it wasn't a light," Bruce said, "but something shiny like tin foil."

"That would make sense," I said. "But wait…a vampire wouldn't line his coffin with tin foil."

"Why not?" June asked.

"Because there would be no reason too. Unless he was a pound of hamburger."

June wiped her forehead as if she were hot. "Maybe the light didn't come from the coffin at all, but from somewhere else."

"Maybe the upstairs light was on," I said.

"Or maybe the vampire used a flashlight, and as long as he kept it away from his face he was fine."

"What does light do to vampires anyway?" Bruce asked.

"Makes them die," I said.

"Like a cross or a stake in the heart," June added, looking at her lobster feet in the stream of water.

* * *

It was Christmas before I dared take the garlic from my pocket. Still, around my neck I wore a cross that my mother had given me for my tenth birthday, and I always made sure that I got home before dark—which my mother loved.

"You are really taking responsibility," she told me one day as I finished the last of the dishes. "I'm proud of you." She put the plate down and gave me a squeeze.

"Thanks," I said, trying to hug her back, but feeling a little awkward in the lie. Was it a lie if you didn't say anything?

Carl was sitting in a chair in the kitchen, reading the newspaper. He nodded his agreement and then went back to his reading. "I thought you'd carry that garlic clove forever," Carl said.

I was surprised Carl knew, and then I realized how bad I must have smelled wearing it. Just one week after Halloween I was getting the brush-off. People would walk by and plug their noses. Some would call me pig pile, others would whisper about me behind my back.

All except for June, that is. She was smelly along with me, although I do believe it bothered her more. Bruce had no idea he smelled so bad. He would walk around the school, and when people told him he smelled he would tell them how much longer he was going to live than they were and that would shut them right up.

Within a week, Bruce had traded the garlic clove for a wooden stake just long enough fit inside his binder, and June had traded her own smell for a cross she'd made out of wood and kept inside her pants pocket.

In the two months since Halloween, not one of us had ventured to the hill and onto the property of Mr. Grant. But we were more determined than ever to stay alive, no matter what anyone said.

# CHAPTER 8

Mr. Green was hanging over the chain-link fence doing something. I had no idea what, until I got closer. The snow was pretty deep that day, almost to my knees, and all I could think about was building a snowman with Bruce and June, but neither of them was home.

It was Friday, and school was out because of winter vacation. And that was my problem. Neither June nor Bruce had told me they were leaving anywhere, but I figured they must have taken a spontaneous journey somewhere without me. I hoped in the deepest part of my soul that the vampire hadn't gotten them.

I told myself that a week before Christmas a person could go anywhere. Except for me, and, of course, Mr. Green, who probably went nowhere anyway because he was so old.

He was pulling a bucket from the piled snow. It was black and had a metal hanger on it, rusted orange.

"I was wondering where this went," he said, turning the bucket upside down and pounding the snow out. A wet wrapper drifted to the snow. "Well, I'll be."

He picked up the brown and silver rectangle and shoved it into his pocket. "Wouldn't be polite to leave it there," he said.

"Samantha..." He winked and handed me the black bucket. "You've come at the right time." He wiped the bucket with a plain white towel he had hidden in his trouser pocket and handed the gift to me.

Only it didn't seem much like a gift, and I wasn't sure what to say. What was I going to do with an old black bucket?

When I grasped the handle, it chilled my hands. I put it before me on the snow and looked up at Mr. Green.

"I think it's your brother's," he said.

"Luke?"

"No, Joshua. The big lad living with you." I almost laughed. But I was more concerned about the bucket. I looked down at the thing sitting on the chilly sidewalk.

"I believe Joshua left it here on Halloween night."

"That's weird."

"I know. A boy like that leaving precious candy for Charlie to eat."

I supposed the "like that" comment was made because Joshua was fat and candy must be the next best thing to heaven, but I didn't say anything. Mr. Green was wearing a thick brown coat with a furry hood. Just his eyes were peeking out. He reminded me suddenly of an Eskimo far away from his homeland.

"Is Charlie all right?"

"Oh, yes…yes. He got a little sick from eating all that candy, but a quick trip to the vet changed all that. He's fine now. But I think I scared him."

"Charlie?"

"No, Joshua."

"I tried to give the bucket back but he was already running up the street."

"Where was Luke?" I asked.

"I don't know," Mr. Green answered. "Can you take it to him? It's been sitting here since October."

I nodded a yes and Mr. Green retreated in the direction of his house. From the pocket of my white coat I pulled my fur muff, but I couldn't hold the handle with it on, so I placed the muff back inside my pocket and carried the bucket home.

The sky was a chalk gray and it looked as if it was going to snow again.

* * *

"That's not my bucket," Joshua said, turning it upside down and glaring at its underneath side.

"Sure it is," I answered. "Mr. Green said so."

Joshua breathed heavily, his belly jiggling along with his chin. "For your information, my black bucket has my name on it. My mother wrote it on there. Don't you think I would recognize my own bucket?"

"It could have worn off," I said. "Mr. Green…"

"I don't care what Mr. Green said." Suddenly, Joshua looked away from me and from the bucket he said wasn't his.

"This is not my bucket." He kicked the thing across the room. It hit smack dab into the dresser leg and stopped face up.

"Well, thanks for nothing," I said, standing up from his stupid bed with the wretched sea creatures swimming on the quilt. "I just thought I'd be nice."

Joshua was silent. He stood up from the opposite end of the bed and walked over to the window. "Thanks anyway," he mumbled.

* * *

"You have a date with your father."

My favorite meal, spaghetti, was being cooked on the stove, but I could hardly think about it, my heart was beating so heavily inside my chest. It had been a long time since I'd seen him. And now, on Christmas Eve he finally wanted to see me?

"When's he coming?"

"What do you mean, when is he coming? He's sitting right there on the couch. Go give him a hug and tell him you'd be glad to go."

I couldn't believe Mother was asking me to hug Daddy. It was a miracle, even if you didn't count the fact that he was here!

I turned the corner from the kitchen, trying to breathe. Perhaps I'd been so busy thinking about Joshua and his stupid bucket that I had completely missed seeing him. Was such a thing possible?

I looked down, fully expecting to see Daddy smiling up at me; instead, Carl was sitting on the couch, and I was momentarily confused. My daddy wasn't here. It was just Carl! And then I knew what my mother meant and I was sorry for having mixed it all up inside my brain.

But was I really sorry? Hadn't I wanted it to be Daddy?

I could hardly look him in the eyes. Dating a married man was not only wrong it was silly. After all, Carl wasn't really my daddy—would never be my daddy.

I tried to smile as he took my hand. "So, what do you think, Samantha? A date?

* * *

"I used to go to church," Carl was saying. I had just taken a bite of shrimp, and it felt very large in my small mouth.

We were sitting in a Chinese restaurant. A light with red tassels hung from the ceiling above us. On the large wall there were various pictures of men and women doing Chinese duties. Red and golden tapestries hung everywhere. Almost every server was Asian except for the one we got, and he'd already left us.

"What?" I mumbled, chewing the last little bit and letting the fish slide down my throat. How had the subject of church come up anyway? Oh, yes—Mother's thoughts about prayer for the true believers—those who didn't sit in row after row of pews pretending to be religious.

"I went as a young boy. Of course, your mother and I don't speak about that time much."

I nodded my understanding and took a drink of root beer. It bubbled at my nose and made me sneeze.

"Bless you," Carl said.

I smiled over at him and reached for a table napkin, wiping the frothy mess against the smooth white material.

"By the way, Mr. Grant brought this over last night." Carl held a black piece of material out across the table. "Recognize this?" he asked, placing the strip of cloth into my shaking hands.

"It looks like June's," I said. "But how…"

My words were drowned by the return of the server. His thin arms reached over the table. "Some water?" he asked. I could barely hear his words. Mr. Grant? The vampire?

"Samantha, you've gone white. Are you sick?"

I looked down at the food that seemed to resemble white lice, pieces of limb, and yellow fingers.

"No…I'm fine," I said. But I wasn't fine at all. Thoughts of the bucket left on Mr. Green's property were suddenly giving me the willies. Had Joshua seen the vampire? Had the vampire come out of his house to bite the neck of my stepbrother? And if so, was Joshua even now a member of the dead?

# CHAPTER 9

"Bruce, I have to talk to you!" I screamed into the phone. After a few rude comments from his mother for waking her up, Bruce had been granted the privilege of talking with me for a few moments. It was nearly three o'clock on Christmas morning, and I hadn't been able to sleep.

"Go back to bed. I'm sure Santa's come," he said sleepily.

I hadn't even thought about the presents. How could I?

"Bruce, listen..." I said into the receiver. "The vampire, Mr. Grant."

"Not him again."

"No...wait! He came to see my father. And you'll never guess what he brought with him!"

"A hickey for your stepfather's neck!"

I breathed heavily into the phone. "No, stupid! June's black sash!" But in the back of my mind I wondered, what if Mr. Grant had also managed to get to Carl?

"What black sash?"

He was still half asleep. "You know, the one she wore on Halloween?"

"The sash? Are you sure?"

"I'm completely sure!"

"Well, that was nice of him."

"Nice of him? Don't you see? If he found the sash and was able to return it to Carl, he must know we were there!"

There was complete silence on the other end of the line and for a moment I thought Bruce had gone back to sleep. And then he said, "I can't believe it, Sam! Mr. Grant, the vampire, knows we saw him!"

\* \* \*

I wasn't too excited that Christmas, even when my mother handed me the medium-large box with the silver wrapping and red bow. The bow came off first, and then I carefully removed the shiny wrapping.

Luke was probably rolling his eyes at me because I was saving the paper. My heart was beating rapidly as I lifted the plain white lid and looked inside.

It was a cat. For a moment I thought it must be real, but then the thing didn't move, and I had the uneasy feeling that if it had been alive, it was surely dead by now. There weren't any breathing holes in the box.

I looked up at my mother. She was smiling widely at me as if hoping I was as joyous about the gift as she was.

Well, I wasn't. I lifted the thing out by the end of its tail. At the bottom of the box was a comb and brush. I looked down at the white cat with the long fur that was meant to be brushed like the real kind. It seemed like a dead thing on my lap, and I suddenly remembered Tiger and Mr. String and Mr. Grant the vampire. Perhaps I'd blamed Mr. String when it hadn't been his fault Tiger was dead.

Thoughts that a vampire like Mr. Grant would kill my cat filled my heart with horror. As I hesitantly unwrapped each of my gifts, I couldn't help but think about Mr. Green's wife—she had passed away just last year. And hadn't Joshua's mother died a few months ago? I had no idea where she lived, but vampires could go anywhere. They weren't hindered by any location, since they could become bats and all.

"Samantha, are you all right?" My mother placed her cold hand on my forehead.

I touched her hand with my own. "I'm fine."

She released her hand, her eyes wide with question, but said nothing. I thought about all the times she'd come to me when I was sick, her cold hand on my forehead, and wished that I was sick now and that I could talk to her about what was in my heart.

"I hope the dinner last night didn't bother your stomach," Carl offered.

I shook my head no, even though I had tasted none of it, my mind too busy thinking about the black sash in front of me. If it had had eyes it would have stared, and if it had had a mouth it would have talked. The sash would have told me about Mr. Grant and when he'd become a vampire. It would have told me what was going to happen to me now that I knew he was one.

I forced a smile. "The dinner was good. It was nice to go out with you...Dad."

Carl smiled and mussed my short brown hair. "No problem, Samantha. We'll have to make it a tradition and do it next Christmas Eve."

"Sure." I placed my white cat on my lap and began to brush its fur even though I didn't like it. The poor, dead thing, I thought. It would have been much better to get a real cat.

My mother and Carl got up from the floor and walked into the kitchen. I was left alone with Joshua, Luke, and the dead cat. After a few moments of complete silence I looked up to see Joshua staring at me, his new truck and miscellaneous clothes and junk scattered around him like a Christmas bazaar.

"What?" I asked him.

He looked down at the yellow truck, a Tonka, and ran it along the floor. He didn't even make the engine noises.

Joshua was too quiet. Actually, he hadn't spoken to me since the bucket incident. He was wearing red pajamas, and no matter where I looked I couldn't see a bite mark. I breathed a sigh of relief. Maybe he'd gotten away in time.

Luke was the same boring brother. He'd torn the Christmas paper like a shredding machine, shrieking at every gift no matter how small. Some things would never change. But then again, some things couldn't help but do just that.

* * *

The water was frozen underneath Bruce's bridge. Small rocks poked through the shiny surface and gave me the feeling of a hidden path below, one that was covered for a time so it might keep secrets.

What was happening with Joshua and the bucket? With Mr. Grant? With my father? Were they vampires now? How could I find out without getting bitten myself? Should I tell Bruce and June, or would they be even more afraid if they knew?

Did I know? I was pretty sure that Joshua had not been bitten; still, the thought occurred to me that I would need to find the entire truth before I shared it. Why get my friends scared for nothing? Still, I had no idea how to find out except to do what I'd done with Joshua: stare very closely for the mark.

My thoughts continued to ramble. I hadn't even received a card from my daddy at Christmas. Was he dead after all? Had the vampire taken him to his house to sleep and bite through countless nights? My mind was filled with little else but Mr. Grant.

Returning to school did little for my happiness. It was near January when I realized that my birthday was close and that once again my daddy wouldn't be there to join me.

Fortunately, I didn't feel completely alone. Bruce was there and so was June. I'd long since forgiven her for sharing her heart with Bruce. It seemed we had an invisible pact, one that no stone or pathway of ice could break. We were friends for life.

# Chapter 10

June hadn't spoken of hypnotizing any of us for months, but now her mouth was bursting forth with the wonders only a hypnotist could perform.

"If we're hypnotized we can do anything!" she said. The ground was cold, and my butt felt like a frozen icicle, but for the second time in my life I truly listened to her ramblings. She'd been right about my new father. I had grown to like him a little more. She'd been somewhat right about my new brother. Although he lied to me about the bucket, I had begun to feel sorry for him.

Wasn't that an improvement over hate? Of course, nothing had happened with Luke. I still couldn't stand him most of the time, but June hadn't hypnotized me about him and so that made sense. The only thing that didn't make sense was the part about me being happy. But maybe being happy was just too large a request even for June.

"…You will not be afraid of the vampire," she was saying. "Together we will capture him and save the world…"

June had decided to hypnotize Bruce and me at the same time. We sat together, our butts frozen solid, our minds opening to new vistas. After her counsel, she would teach us how to do the same for her.

\* \* \*

Bruce was laughing. The sky was as black as a chalkboard and I should have been home. June had left us in a fit and I wasn't sure if either of us would ever see her again.

"I can't believe you snorted," he said.

Well, I always snorted when I laughed too hard and so I said, "Well, at least I didn't fart!"

Bruce's scar lit up beet red as he laughed. "I couldn't help it," he said. "All that time sitting on the ground, it was held in, you know."

"It should have been frozen," I said.

"Ha, ha, ha."

"Well…" I giggled, "we'll just have to protect June, that's all."

"Sure, but how?"

I thought a lot about Bruce's question but couldn't answer it. I knew that somehow Bruce and I were protected because of June's words, but she would never be because of us. The words had come awkwardly from my lips. I couldn't say more than two of them without bending over in laughter. And then Bruce had tried with little success.

"You will not be…" he had begun, only to fart into the air, like a car's exhaust pipe. I had started to laugh and then Bruce joined me. And that was that.

Tomorrow was Sunday. Usually June went to church. Bruce and I didn't go, so we would spend a few hours together without her. She could never join us on Sunday, and I tried to understand that her father was religious and everything, but I couldn't quite work it out in my brain. I wondered what they could be teaching you in a church that would keep you from your friends on Sunday, but I never dared ask. It was like another secret was being kept from me, under the bridge, in between the brown and black rocks in Bruce's yard.

\* \* \*

It was evening when I heard Luke screaming at me from his bedroom, but I wasn't going to budge. I was reading a book about vampires and didn't want to be bothered. But the call came again, more piercing than the first, so I relented and walked to the door. There, lying sprawled on the bedroom carpet, his face to the floor, was Joshua. He looked like a beached whale.

Luke looked up at me with tears in his eyes. "Go get Mom! I think she's outside!"

"What's wrong?"

"Josh…he fell. He just fell!"

"From the bed?"

55

"No, dummy! Go get Mom!"

For a moment I hesitated, taking in the scene of Joshua, his face kissing the carpet, and Luke, his brown eyes screaming for help. And then I fled.

I tripped only once on the old green carpet separating the living room from the kitchen, but my body slid to the door and clunked to a stop. I stood, holding my head. With my left hand I opened the wooden door and the metal screen and plunged outside.

"Mom! Mom!"

She wasn't in the front yard, so I fled to the back. But she wasn't there either. "Mom! Mom!" I screamed.

Suddenly, as if from the depths of a great pit, I heard a voice. "She took a casserole over to Mr. Grant."

I looked up, tears streaming down my cheeks, and saw Mr. String waving at me. I looked down at the grass, pretending not to have seen him, and continued to call, "Mom! Mom!"

I ran to the opposite end of the house, the side where Luke and Joshua slept, but my mother wasn't there either. Returning to the front of the house I met Mr. String. "Something is wrong," he said.

"No…" I answered, shaking my head like a fake wind-up toy.

"Has something happened?"

I nodded.

"In the house?"

Without another word he brushed me aside and entered the house. I followed him, so numb I couldn't have felt anything more if I had tried.

"Where are they?" he asked, his heavy arms swinging against his sides.

"Down there…the first door on the left…"

He raced down the hall and entered the room, but I didn't want to watch. I turned my back just as he entered Luke's room.

When the paramedics arrived I was still sitting on the old green couch where Mother had told us about the divorce. Mother hadn't returned from Mr. Grant's, and it had been half an hour at least.

Mr. String sat down next to me, his large feet making dirty marks on my mother's newly vacuumed floor. He patted my back.

"It's going to be all right," he whispered. "Don't worry."

How could I tell him that I was more worried about my mother than my stupid stepbrother? If he'd already been bitten, he was lost…but my mother…

As if reading my thoughts, Mr. String said, "I'm going to get your mother. Can you call your father and let him know what's happened?"

I figured Mr. String meant Carl. Only I had no idea what I was supposed to tell him when he answered. I dialed the number anyway.

"Franklin Real Estate," the woman on the other end said after only two rings.

"Yes, I mean, is my…I mean, is Carl there?"

"Carl Matthews?"

"No. Carl…Gregory."

The last name sounded foreign to me. I had written it on all of my school papers since the adoption, but it still felt like I was making it up.

"Just a moment please."

I waited. And waited. From the back room I could hear squealing and yelling. Was Joshua dead?

"Hello?"

"Ah…Dad…Carl…um, Joshua is sick," I said, trying to breathe.

"Sick? What's he got?"

"I…don't know. The guys that help you breathe are here."

"What guys? Samantha, what are you talking about?"

"You know, the guys that come in the ambulance?"

There was a heavy click.

# CHAPTER 11

My mother returned without a mark on her. I looked up at her neck as she walked through the kitchen and into the living room. When she sat down on the old green couch I sat next to her and looked more closely. Nothing.

It was nine o'clock and way past bedtime, but no one seemed to care. Joshua was breathing fairly easily now, but by the looks of him he wouldn't be eating candy bars for a very long time.

Mr. String had returned home and Luke wouldn't speak to me. He sat in his room crying—something I had rarely seen him do. Joshua was sitting across from me in the cushioned chair with the wicker back. He seemed to be in a daze as he watched the conversation. I couldn't see a single mark on his thick neck.

Mother was frantic. "How could Luke do such a thing?" she said.

*Luke?* I thought wildly to myself.

Carl was sitting on the other side of my mother. He had his arm around her. A strange sensation traveled up my spine as I thought of them together, and then it was gone. "I don't think he meant it," Carl said.

"It's a miracle Joshua's not dead!"

"The miracle is that the paramedics were able to get here in time."

My mother nodded and looked at me. "Joshua's frightened Samantha to death," she said.

"Not quite," my father answered.

I guess he meant it as a joke but my mother didn't laugh. She turned to Joshua. "How are you feeling now?" she asked.

"Fine," Joshua gulped. "I'm sorry to have caused so much trouble. I didn't mean to eat all of Luke's candy."

I was furious with Luke, and I was angry with Joshua for giving in to him. Here I'd thought Joshua had struggled for his life with a vampire when all along he'd been choking on those candy bars stuffed into his fat cheeks!

* * *

Luke was watching me from inside the living room window, his face smushed up close in a frozen position. It was a Monday, one day before my birthday, and Luke wasn't going to be let out of his cage until the following Tuesday.

I was outside in the front yard and Joshua was beside me, trying to carry on a conversation. I wasn't listening. I was thinking of Luke. Why would he force Joshua to do such a terrible thing?

As Luke's eyes pierced my own from the other side of the window, I was suddenly struck by how much we really looked alike. I hated to admit it, but even Luke's hair color looked the same as mine—like mushy brown dirt. My hair wasn't much different from his, except that I brushed it. His small hands pressed against the window like a cat's paws, and I could see the clouds of breath left over from his blowing on the window.

He really wanted to be out here. Or maybe I should have been in there like a good sister, but the morning after the choking episode I'd seen Joshua stuffing another juicy morsel into his wet cheeks. I pretended I didn't see him, just like now, even though I wanted to talk with him in the worst possible way.

Finally he got my attention when he said, "Sam, I'm sorry I lied."

I couldn't believe it. I looked at him, really looked at him, and asked, "You going to tell me about the bucket?"

He nodded his head.

"So…!"

"It's kind of hard," he mumbled, a dark brown ooze coming from his lips.

"Do it anyway," I said.

"I gotta sit," he said, and plunked himself down on the front lawn. Fortunately, the snow had cleared and there was nothing but cool grass scrunching against my butt.

Across the street I could hear a few of the neighbors talking near their cars; next door the air was silent.

"That bucket was so full of candy you wouldn't believe it," he started, looking down at the grass and pulling one green tendril from the earth's crust. "I was at Mr. Green's and we were talking."

"Who was talking?"

"Me and Luke. Well, until he went home."

"Why?" I felt like a lawyer on a cop show but I didn't care.

"We had a fight."

"About what?"

Joshua looked at me, a big tear streaking down his cheek. "He said I was fat."

All I could think in that instant was, so what? Everyone knows you're fat.

"He said he couldn't hang out with me anymore," Joshua sniffed, "and then he dumped my candy right there in front of Mr. Green's house."

"Was anyone else with you?" I asked.

"Lots of kids." He looked away from me and continued, "Last night when I choked, I only took that candy because Luke dared me to. He said if I did it he would be my friend again."

I couldn't believe it. "Why would you want to be Luke's friend anyway?" I asked, glad that at last someone besides myself had seen my brother's true colors. Had I actually thought warmly of him a moment before?

"He's the only person besides my mom that has ever been nice to me. And now…she's gone."

It seemed I suddenly had a huge piece of chocolate candy stuck inside my throat, and for the first time ever I had no idea what to say. Joshua, however, was talking fast and furiously. I don't think anything I might have said would have stopped him.

"…My father, our…father, he wasn't always such a good dad like he is now. When my mom and him were first married they yelled at each other a lot. Sometimes he would throw things. And once, he hit Mom in the face."

I wasn't sure that I wanted to hear any more but I listened anyway.

"Mom and Dad went to marriage counseling for a long time. And then one day when I thought things had finally ended, I came home to find my mom rocking back and forth in the corner of her room. It was like she was rocking a baby, only she didn't have a baby, only herself.

"Later, Dad came home. She was still in her room, not rocking but sitting real quiet in the corner. When he tried to lift her up she started crying like a baby. Next thing I knew he was carrying her to the bed and yelling at me to leave the room. Like somehow I had caused it."

Joshua sniffed. "After that night Mom was taken away. I saw her on weekends for a long time. And then one night Dad called me into his room and told me she had died in her sleep."

"Oh," I said, hardly believing what I heard, but believing it at the same time. I figured Joshua's mother must have gone to one of those nut houses with bars on the windows and locks on the bedroom doors.

"I heard you had a dog," I said, trying to change the subject. "Your daddy was talking about him one night with my mother—our mother."

"Yeah. A good old dog, Chipper. When Mom left he sort of left too."

I looked into Joshua's sand-colored eyes. They were filled with tears; one drop and then another fell from his eyes and onto his grungy pants. "Chipper, he kept running away. The last time…we couldn't find him. I didn't want to come here," he added, looking far away toward where his home used to be.

I nodded, unsure of how I should respond to this aching boy's heart. I had never heard anything so terrible in my life. Even my own life seemed better in comparison.

I put my arm around his heavy shoulders and we sat there for a long time. When Joshua stopped crying he looked over at me and smiled. "Thank you," he said.

I nodded, warmth traveling up the back of my spine and melting into my heart.

\* \* \*

I'd never cried on my birthday. Not once. Of course, there's a first time for everything.

The box from my mother revealed a new sweater—bright red, and just what I'd wanted from the department store window. Carl was

61

grinning widely as I opened my gift from him. It was a horn for my new bike.

I honked it once, twice, and then thanked him.

Joshua handed over his package. It was wrapped in smiley face wrapping paper. What appeared to be chocolate stains caressed some of the characters' faces, making them look like they had real beards.

I ripped the paper, and my mother gasped. Eight candy bars fell to my lap. "No more of those," Joshua said.

"You sneak!" Luke screamed. "Give them to me!"

I huddled around the candy like a snake around its prey. "They're mine!" I shrieked back.

"I bought them with my own money!" Joshua yelled.

After a few moments of grasping without success, Joshua's words began to sink in, and then Luke asked me politely, "Sam, let me see."

"You promise not to steal them?"

Luke nodded. He searched through the bars with his skinny fingers. "Sorry," he said at last, looking over at Joshua and then at me. "Sorry, Sam."

Josh smiled. So did Mother and Carl. Carl patted my hand. I didn't care.

"My turn," Luke said.

He placed a box on my lap and waited for the first rip. I looked down at the box. It was the same size as a shoebox. What would Luke be doing buying me a pair of shoes? Maybe they were slippers. I needed slippers.

"Hurry up!"

"OK." I tore the wrapping and looked inside. What I saw wasn't even close to shoes. I couldn't have been more surprised if I'd gotten another dead cat.

I held up the metal spoons from Mother's kitchen drawer—except these spoons were crusted with dried dirt. Some of the dirt was even splattered in clods on the bottom of the box.

"My spoons!" Mother shrieked.

"I didn't want you to forget," Luke said, completely ignoring Mother and grinning over at me. "I miss spending time with you, Sis."

I placed the box on the carpet and crawled over to him. A piece of hair from the back of his head was sticking straight up like Dennis the Menace's, but I didn't care.

"Thank you, Luke," I said, a small tear escaping my left eye.

Luke smiled back and scrunched up my hair. I didn't fix it.

In the end, Mother let me keep one of the spoons. The rest she washed thoroughly and put back in the kitchen drawer.

I left my spoon out—dirt and all. It meant something deep to me, something so far down in the earth that, at first, I just couldn't explain it. It was as if whenever I saw that shiny spoon lying there, with its accompanying dirt, I just couldn't help but be reminded of Luke and his love for me.

\* \* \*

"I'm sorry. Really sorry," I told June on Monday. We were sitting in class and June was behind me.

"Greenland is an icy world. Other than the coastline..." Mrs. Henry was saying, but it was hard to concentrate. All I could feel was June's heavy breath on my neck and the loud tapping of her pencil.

Finally, I turned, more scared than I'd like to admit, but ready to get the whole thing over with. June stared at me evilly as I opened my mouth to say my apologies. In the middle of her tongue was a piece of candy—red—and she held it within her tongue's hollow like a pond of water. Her red hair was pulled back tightly and her blue eyes didn't even wink.

"June..." I began. She blinked and looked away.

"During the winter months the weather is quite cold, but as the summer approaches, the life of the country..." Mrs. Henry droned.

"June!" I tapped her arm.

"Leave me alone!" she muttered between clenched teeth. June had her eyes riveted on Mrs. Henry, as if she were interested, which I was sure she was not. How could she be interested in something so boring?

I turned myself forward, breathing heavily because of June's rudeness, and tried to concentrate on the teacher. I couldn't.

Hadn't I forgiven her countless times for spreading evil gossip about me? Hadn't I allowed her to be my friend? To spend time with

63

me? So, I'd laughed during Bruce's hypnotism of her. He *had* farted, you know. How could she hate me for that?

# CHAPTER 12

"Girls are stupid," Bruce said. We were sitting on the small bridge, allowing our feet to dangle over the ice that was beginning to thin. It was early March, and the wind blew in cool streaks across my cheeks, but I wasn't shivering. Through the winter season my thoughts had become wiser.

I knew I wasn't the only one hurting from the separation of a parent. Joshua was hurting too. I knew that Luke had changed somehow—he wasn't the mean brother I'd made him out to be—and that a grown-up could be a friend, even if he was a grown-up like Mr. Green.

I did little sitting on the ground now, but the boards of the bridge were almost as bad. Last week I'd had to pull out a sliver from my back end, using the mirror in my bedroom as my eyes. The piece of wood felt like a huge bite from some unknown predator, but when I pulled the thing out it was only a little thicker than a piece of thread. I dropped it to the ground like belly button lint and looked at my bottom with the red mark, pulled up my panties, and promptly forgot all about it.

Until now...

I've often heard talk from grown-ups about adults calling other adults a pain in the backside, except they don't use the word backside, and I wondered if that's what June had turned out to be in my life. A pain in the "you know what."

I hadn't talked to June in more than two weeks. She'd begun to hang out with a girl named Tracey, who was perfect in every sense of the word that you can imagine. She was beautiful and attracted the attention of every boy she walked by. She smiled at just the right time, which was every time I saw her, and she got good grades and never seemed to do anything wrong. Everyone liked her. But then I imagined a lot as I watched June and Tracey eat lunch together and walk home from school together without me.

Fortunately, I had Bruce, and perhaps I always would. He was watching me now, his brows crinkling up like an empty potato chip bag.

"Have you heard anything about Mr. Grant lately?" I asked.

"No. You?"

"Nothing. I told you about the casserole, didn't I?"

"Yeah, that's pretty weird. How's your brother doing?"

"If you mean Joshua, he's doing all right, I guess. I think he and Luke should make up."

"You and June should make up. I don't think she's mad anymore."

Just this morning on the way to class June had glared at me, so I didn't know what Bruce was thinking. June and I would never be friends again unless she made the effort first.

"I heard her talking to that new friend of hers—Tracey, I think. She was saying something about you—how long you'd been friends and stuff. She talked like she wanted to be friends with you again."

I strongly doubted that but nodded my head at Bruce. After all, he was trying to help, so why shouldn't I let him?

When he reached out his left hand to hold mine I took it. My hand cradled inside his, and I thought, all warm and glowing, about the kiss at the beginning of the summer. He hadn't kissed me since then, and it was almost the end of my fifth-grade year. I wondered how long I'd have to wait.

* * *

Luke and Joshua were as separate as oil from water. I figured they must have made up some sort of deal to get them through the rest of the school year, the deal leaning heavily in Luke's favor. I'd seen special pacts made with cut fingers and mixed blood and wondered if Joshua had had the courage to make such a promise to Luke. Probably not. More than likely Luke had just told Joshua to bug off or something.

Luke was hanging out with a bunch of guys I didn't know. If it had been Joshua I would have been worried the guys were playing him for a fool. Joshua would never be able to hang out with the cool crowd—unless he lost weight, of course. But Luke, well, he just seemed to fit in somehow.

I wondered if Joshua would ever fit in anywhere. I wondered if I would ever fit into the life of June again. She and Tracey were still friends. I would hear them giggling in the corner of the lunchroom, and whispering behind their hands as I walked by.

On Saturday, I watched as Tracey knocked on June's door and June let her in. I was angry then and confused at what I'd seen. I wanted to run over there and yank all of June's hair out. I wanted to swear mean cussing words at her and call her a horse's "you know what." But I didn't.

Sometimes I'd head to the school playground after hours and swing alone, allowing my short brown hair to rise through the air, my feet to sweep up the dirt between the indentations of my tennis shoes. And then I would cry about all the things I'd lost.

Mother. Daddy. And now June. I wondered when I would like myself again. Hadn't I once? When Daddy was here? Was the memory of Daddy already becoming a blur?

Would I ever feel like myself again? Maybe someday I would feel at peace. I would laugh again—really laugh. I wouldn't hate my mother for divorcing Daddy. I wouldn't be mad at Carl for trying to take his place. I wouldn't hate Luke for sharing me with someone else. But most of all, I wouldn't hate me.

* * *

Mr. Green was working outside. I had just finished my chores, and Mother had allowed me to go outside and play. Except I didn't want to play. It was Saturday, and Joshua had gone with his father to a movie. Luke was over at Steven String's house and my mother was cleaning the house as usual. I didn't dare ride over to June's.

As I stood beyond the chain-link fence I watched Mr. Green work, his heavy body bent over to pull one weed and then another. He was whistling something between his dentures and I wondered what the song was—it seemed as though the noisy air had become still and solemn. Finally, he stood as straight as possible. Mr. Green

67

turned to the fence where I was standing. He smiled over at me. "Well, Samantha, what brings you my way?"

I smiled back, not knowing what to say. Bruce wasn't home and there wasn't anyone left to talk to but Mr. Green.

Mr. Green opened the gate. I walked in.

Now I knew what was wrong. I couldn't hear his dog, Charlie. The yard was as silent as a funeral.

"Where is Charlie?" I asked.

Mr. Green led me to a chair on the back porch. It was made of painted green metal and rocked back and forth on a sort of stand that was bent like someone kneeling. He sat across from me on one exactly like it. Tears began to fill his eyes, and when they ran down his whiskery cheeks he did not wipe them away.

"Charlie was sick, you know."

I didn't know. He seemed to bark healthily enough to me and had scared me so much on Halloween last year that I'd practically wet my pants. But I didn't say the same to Mr. Green; actually, I didn't say anything.

"I took him to the vet. Cancer, they said."

"I'm sorry." I didn't know a dog could get cancer. I didn't know that dogs died of anything but old age. Perhaps Mr. Grant had come by and sucked the life out of him and the vet only thought he'd had cancer.

"Over there…" Mr. Green pointed to a thick brush of weeds that might have been a garden the year before. He stood. "Come over here and see," he said.

I stood, but I didn't want to. I hoped that the dog had already been buried and that his body wouldn't be lying there decaying right in front of me.

Mr. Green stopped at the edge of the grass and pointed again. "See the spot where I've cleared?"

Sure enough, there was a bald spot amongst the weeds, as bare as an old guy's head. And underneath that spot I could visualize his dog, Charlie, buried.

"It was hard finding a box large enough," Mr. Green said. "A shoe box just wouldn't have worked," you know.

I nodded, trying to picture that big old Doberman inside a small shoebox. It just wouldn't have been as possible as spoons.

"Finally, I went to the market," he said. "I picked up an apple box, brought it home and tried fitting Charlie in there. Charlie was too snug a fit. I finally settled on an old refrigerator box, cut down a bit, of course."

I looked down at the spot and took it all in like a grand camera they use to produce movies. I wanted to remember everything. The spot where the dog was, how the weeds looked surrounding his buried body, even the face of Mr. Green as he looked down at Charlie's home for eternity. I wanted to remember it all. I don't know why, but maybe I never wanted to be there myself and I felt that maybe if I looked long and hard at the spot I could tell my body that I never wanted to be down in the ground like Charlie. And maybe, just maybe, it would listen.

# CHAPTER 13

It was late March when I finally got a smile from June. She walked up to me and pulled me aside. I was nearing the classroom door, anxious for some freedom I probably wouldn't even get at home.

My thoughts were on Mother. She wasn't proud of me. At least not this year. So far my grades were low but passing. But I didn't care. And neither, it seemed, did my new father, Carl.

Mother said he was busy at work; she said that money had become a little tight and that all of Carl's energy had gone to his job. For the first time since her marriage I had begun to see pain in my mother's eyes, and it comforted me. It was like we were the same: feeling pain, but not at all sure how to change it.

Why couldn't things be the way they used to be? Why did I have to feel so scattered? Why the daily doubts and fears…the loneliness even when others were around me?

June leaned toward my left ear and whispered something that at first I didn't hear. When she whispered it again, I turned to her with disbelief in my eyes. What she'd told me was surprising.

"My friend Tracey is getting baptized."

"What do you mean, baptized?" The only thing I knew about that word was the connection it had with little babies, a priest, and some sprinkling of water on the baby's head.

"You know, in the water and stuff."

I thought I knew what she meant about the water, though it was hard for me to imagine a girl getting sprinkled on the head like a baby. I was confused about her meaning of "and stuff." And although I didn't know what to say next, June helped me out by talking all the way home.

"She's going to be a Mormon. She has to go to church every week now, and partake of the Sacrament and go to Primary…"

My head felt like a fried egg when she'd finished, and I'd understood less than half of the words from her busy mouth.

In my room I thought them over. Baptism. Confirmation. Some gift called the Holy Ghost. And what did it mean that she'd been inactive? And that Tracey wasn't a member? Her last words as she'd stepped away from my door were truly surprising. "Tracey wants you to come. She feels bad that we've been mad at each other."

I couldn't imagine what I'd possibly do at a baptism. I just couldn't imagine the priest holding up Tracey, even though she probably wasn't too heavy, and sprinkling water on the top of her head.

* * *

Bruce was laughing. "You mean you didn't know June was a Mormon?"

"No," I said, telling him the complete truth. What I knew about June's religious life was that she went to church on Sunday. How could a person know about someone's religion if they never spoke of it?

"Well, she's a Mormon all right. Her dad's one too. Kind of makes you wonder why she loves doing that hypnotism stuff so much, doesn't it?"

"They probably do it in their church," I said.

Bruce nodded, the understanding showing in his eyes. "You're probably right," he answered. "Once when I was peeking through her window, there were all of these guys standing around June's father with their hands on his head. June's father was sitting in the middle of them. A few minutes later the men moved away and June's father stood and shook all of their hands."

"Weird," I said. "What do you think they were doing?"

"Probably some kind of hypnotism thing," he said. "June's father scares me. Once he yelled at me for being inside his trailer."

"Why?" I asked. "You weren't kissing June, were you?" The words were out before I could stop them.

Bruce looked at me and blushed. "Of course not!" he said.

"Then why would he yell at you?"

Bruce shrugged his shoulders. "I don't know," he said.

My heart was thumping wildly. Well, the least he could do was tell me the truth—or say he was sorry or something. But Bruce said nothing, and after a while he changed the subject and we began to talk about something else.

* * *

June handed me an invitation. On it was the date of Tracey's baptism, April 2, and the year—1971. Underneath the date was Tracey's full name: Tracey Lavina Carlson. Beneath her name was the time and place: 7 P.M., Golden West Ward. On the back was a scripture reference that read "1 Nephi 3:7."

I thanked June and shoved the piece of paper into my pocket, never intending to do anything but throw it in the garbage when I got home. But her next words surprised me.

"I'm sorry, Sam."

Her blue eyes melted into mine and for a moment I could see her pain. And then she said, "I never should have gotten mad at you. Since I've been going to church I have learned a lot of things."

I couldn't imagine what June had learned recently, seeing as how she'd always gone to church, but I tried to listen anyway.

"And I need to tell you something." She hesitated for only a moment, her thoughts searching her mind. "I know that the church is true."

A small spark of something shot up my back and was gone.

"Bruce said you're a Mormon. How come you never told me?"

June looked down at the cement step, and then up at my face. "I haven't always been a true Mormon," she said.

Well, what was that supposed to mean—a true Mormon? But I decided not to ask; June was continuing her words, so fortunately I didn't have to.

"You know on Sunday when I said I was going to church?"

I nodded and suddenly my heart was pounding within me.

"I wasn't."

"So where did you go?" I asked.

"Promise you won't hate me," June asked.

"I promise."

"Well, my father took me to the doctor."

A sudden thought of cancer came to my mind, and then the creepy fangs of Mr. Grant. I looked at June's neck but couldn't see a mark.

"He's a certain kind of doctor. He helps with stuff besides broken bones."

"Oh," I replied, trying to imagine a doctor that didn't fix things.

"He's a psychiatrist."

"You mean those guys that get into the brains of crazy people?"

I shouldn't have said it. June started to cry. "I knew I shouldn't have told you," she said, turning the doorknob. But I reached for her arm and pulled her back to me.

"I didn't mean it," I said. "How long have you been going?"

"Eight months." She wiped away a stray tear. "I was so mad when you laughed at me. Hypnotizing you guys was never a joke to me," she said. "After that happened, I knew I could never tell you the truth."

"About you seeing a psychiatrist."

June nodded. She left me on the steps and walked to the green lawn. Sitting down, she began to play with the grass blades and began to sing. It was the same tune Mr. Green had sung only two days before!

My hands began to shake, but I was sure it was because I knew the truth even before she'd spoken the words.

"I've been going to see Mr. Green at his office."

"It can't be Mr. Green!" I said, looking directly into her eyes. "He's old and never goes anywhere!"

She was momentarily surprised. "For your information, he has an office downtown, and he isn't as old as you think."

"You're joking," I said.

"No."

I was silent then as I took in everything I had heard from June. "I guess you know that his dog is dead," I said, trying to change the subject.

She nodded.

"I'm really sorry," she said. "Especially about hypnotizing you guys as if I knew what I was doing."

"Well, maybe you did know," I said.

She smiled. "Mr. Green has been hypnotizing me. He says it will help me to discover why I've been so depressed."

"Your mother left," I said.

"Yeah. But I don't seem to be able to get over it," June offered, making me think of my own struggles with a father who wanted nothing to do with me either.

\* \* \*

I don't know why I dressed up for the baptism, but I did. Maybe it was because June had asked me special, and I was suddenly feeling a new bond with her. I couldn't believe that I hadn't known she was sick. I couldn't believe she hadn't told me about going to see a psychiatrist when we were supposed to be friends. But somehow, I could imagine that I would have done the same thing.

How much had I shared with her about my daddy leaving me? How much did she know about my feelings of loneliness? Or my feelings about my new father and brother?

I had to admit she knew very little mainly because I didn't want her spreading it to the entire world. Well, maybe she wouldn't have. Maybe she would have kept it as secret as the feelings she had about herself.

The music in the room was so soothing I almost fell asleep. But I tried to remain awake as Tracey sat in a folding chair ahead of me, talking to a man. She had a white pajama outfit on that must have been a jumpsuit. But it looked more like a pajama outfit and I tried not to laugh.

No one else was laughing at them, even the man sitting next to her who may have been Tracey's father. But he was dressed as she was except his suit was larger and tighter against his stomach.

Next to the man sat a woman with blond hair and four other children, two girls and two boys, dressed really nicely, like they were going to a fancy restaurant or something. I looked down at my plain blue dress and wished I hadn't worn it. Still, the dress had been a Christmas gift from Carl. He said I looked pretty in it.

June was sitting next to me and she was wearing a black Gunne Sax dress with various flowers spreading their leaves across the dark fabric. For those of you who don't know, a Gunne Sax dress was the best of the best. There were many different prints, but all the dresses had beautifully sculpted collars and matching hems. Sometimes the sleeves were short, like the one June was wearing. The one I wanted was blue with yellow flowers. It had long sleeves.

But none of that seemed to matter to June as I watched her watch Tracey. In front of Tracey and her family was a large bathtub, sort of like a swimming pool but smaller, with small turquoise squares on the bottom and partway up the sides. Water was already in the small pool and I wondered if it was warm.

Soothing music was still coming from the piano in the back of the room when a gray-haired man in a black suit and striped tie stood up in front of the group.

"I am Bishop McMillan," he said. "Welcome to Tracey Carlson's baptism. We are happy she has chosen to be baptized."

A sudden feeling struck me, and I wanted to wave it away, but it lingered long after Tracey had been put under the water by the man in white and had come back up, her hair stuck to her head, water dripping from her body. Even after I returned home to a silent mother and a stepfather staring unblinking at the television set, the warm feeling lingered on like Christmas.

I walked to my room with the warm feeling in my heart and went through the small purple trash can. I sorted through old gum wrappers, school assignments, and one banana peel. Near the bottom of the barrel I found the invitation that had all but engraved itself in my mind—well, all except for the scripture bit that I hadn't wanted to look up.

I went to the living room and lifted the old family Bible from the bottom shelf and returned to my bedroom. The book was bound in black leather and the word "Bible" was deeply engraved on the cover with golden letters. It was quite heavy. Opening the first page, I saw a bunch of names: those of my father, mother, brother, grandmothers, grandfathers, and people beyond them I didn't even know.

Each entry was written delicately with a thin black pen, in the handwriting of the person recording at the time. I wondered what my mother would do now that we had a different daddy, but the thought didn't last long as I turned the crisp pages to the heading that read: "The Holy Bible containing the Old and New Testaments translated out of the original tongues…"

"Original tongues." Now that was funny. Perhaps there were fake ones too! I turned the page. Some letter to Prince James stared me in the face. Well, that was for the prince. I turned the page.

75

"The names and order of all the books of the Old and New Testaments," it read.

Unfolding the invitation given to me by June, I looked over the reference: "1 Nephi 3:7."

"Genesis, Exodus, Leviticus…" I scanned down the first long column of names and started up the second. "…Ecclesiastes, The Song of Solomon…" and down both columns of "The Books of the New Testament and Appendix," which made me laugh again.

I knew the appendix meant the back of the book, not the stringy stuff inside your body that I'd learned about in school, but almost every other name I came across I knew nothing about. And I couldn't even find the word "Nephi."

What strange scripture was this?

# CHAPTER 14

Joshua was crying. The door to Joshua's room was open, but I had a feeling that something was wrong. As I stopped in the doorway I realized I was right. Joshua was lying on his bed with the great whale printed on it, sobbing into his pillow.

I was frustrated about not being able to find the scripture reference the day before, and now someone I was beginning to care about was sobbing in front of me. I watched Joshua for a moment. Watched as he wiped his eyes. Watched his belly shuddering like Jell-O, and his mouth twitching with pain. When I decided to come in and comfort him he was already waving me to his bed.

I sat. He wiped his nose. I tried not to watch as the slime dried on his thick arms. But in only moments I was intent on his story and the worry was gone.

"Luke hates me," he began, taking me back to the day he'd told me the terrible truth about his mother losing her mind.

"He couldn't hate you…" I began, but I was cut off.

"Oh, he hates me all right. Yesterday, when you were gone to that baptism, we had a fight." So that's why Mother hadn't acknowledged my return and Carl had been glued to the television set. Actually, I hadn't seen my brother since my return and wondered if he was in the same state of mind—crying somewhere alone.

And yet, I couldn't believe my brother would cry.

"I told him."

He paused for only a moment.

"I told Luke that my mother had committed suicide. Dad got real mad! He began to yell at Luke. He told him to go to his room. After that, Luke wouldn't speak to me. He called me…"

"Wait!" I interrupted. "You told me your mother died in her sleep!"

"I lied."

I took a deep breath.

"That's OK, Joshua," I said, patting him on the arm, because suddenly it didn't matter that he'd lied to me.

"Will you hug me?" he asked. Up to that day I'd done nothing more than touch him briefly in comfort. Maybe I surprised Joshua as well as myself when I relented.

The hug was mushy but I felt warmth spreading from the bottom of my feet to the back of my neck. I held him until the sobs stopped, until he released himself from my arms. And after he thanked me, I left his room and returned to the note crumpled within my trash can. I read it once more, wondering what the reference meant.

* * *

"Stay away from Joshua," I said.

Luke was playing over at Steven's. It was past dinnertime, almost eight o'clock. In another hour the skies would be as dark as the pit underneath the swimming pool where Bruce and I had first kissed.

I was mad at Luke—madder than I had ever been before. For two weeks I'd worked through the words that I would tell him. And I hadn't crossed out the swearwords. But today, the fifteenth of March, I wondered if I could say them. I wondered if I would be able to carry out the plan.

Luke and Joshua were not speaking to each other. Obviously, it was Carl's fault they were not speaking to each other—he'd yelled first—but now Luke stayed as far away from Joshua as a diver would from a shark. It just wasn't fair to Joshua. He needed a friend, but there was no way Luke was going to get near him right now if I could help it. And then it had come to me. Maybe all Luke needed was a scare of his own—a scare as terrible as suicide.

Luke was laughing and Steven was joining in like some sorry chorus.

"You brought your bodyguard, huh?" Luke said.

I couldn't understand why Luke's niceness to me on my birthday had suddenly turned to evil just because Joshua had finally had the courage to tell him the truth.

Bruce was standing quietly beside me, but I could feel his anger too. I'd told him everything about Joshua's father and mother, and how badly Luke was treating Joshua because of what he knew. If my mother found out what I was going to do now, she wouldn't understand. She was still mad about something, and I didn't even care. All I cared about was helping to heal Joshua.

"Promise that you won't hurt Joshua again," I said, pointing my finger at him like mother would.

Steven smiled and punched Luke on the arm. "Yeah," he chuckled, "promise your sister."

Luke spit on the ground. "What do you think I am, some sissy?"

"Yeah," I said.

"Prove it," he answered.

"Close your eyes," I ordered.

"Stupid," he said. "I'm not going to do that."

"Then you're saying you're a sissy?"

"No. I'm just not dumb enough to close my eyes."

"I guess you don't trust your sister," Bruce said.

Luke closed his eyes.

"Go in the house, Steven," Bruce said.

"Now who's the sissy?" Luke muttered under his breath. "Steven stays."

Bruce nodded. "We can do what we need to do with him here."

"Put your hands out!"

"You're going to tie his hands!" Steven exclaimed. "I'm going to tell my mom!"

"Shut up!" Luke railed at his friend. His eyes were still shut. "This might be interesting."

Bruce pulled a thick strand of rope from inside the back of his shirt and tied my brother's hands. "We'll need your help anyway," he said to Steven.

Luke opened his eyes. "I've changed my mind," he said, but the rope was already tied around his wrists and no amount of shaking would loose them.

"Take his legs!" Bruce barked.

I grabbed for Luke's legs. They were kicking as fast as a propeller on the back of a boat. But Luke had changed a few plans.

"Steven! Grab his legs!"

Steven hesitated for only an instant, and then he reached for Luke's legs. In a moment, and after a few kicks to Steven's arms and stomach, Luke's legs were securely held together by the rope.

"Take his middle!" Bruce said.

I did as I was told. But Luke's eyes were open and he was angry now. "Let me go!" he screamed.

Steven started to laugh. "Are we going to drop him in the mud?" he asked.

"No," I answered, although the thought had some merit. "Something far worse."

\* \* \*

Luke screamed almost the entire trip to Mr. Grant's house. Fortunately, Bruce had remembered to bring his mother's flowered scarf with him. Luke's mouth was tied shut, sort of like a horse with a bit, only he couldn't even whinny when Bruce was finished.

The skies above were just beginning to shelter us with gray, and I felt within my soul that same cool gray feeling, but I tried to ignore it. We were doing the right thing; there wasn't anything we could do but this. The discussion with Bruce had been heated at times, but finally we'd decided on the answer. June would have hated this adventure, but we were still separate from one another for the most part, although she was nice enough to me when she saw me.

It was like she was suddenly too good for me. As if the mere thought of spending time with me drew her into evil. Well, she may have had second thoughts about what we were going to do with Luke now.

At Mr. Grant's house we put Luke down and untied his feet. He kicked Steven in the stomach, and before we could stop him, Steven had gone wailing home. We needed to work fast.

Taking Luke by the shoulder, Bruce half pushed, half led Luke to the bottom of the outside cement stairs to Mr. Grant's basement. Luke moved his head back and forth in anger and tried to release his hands, but Bruce had tied them tightly behind him.

"Check the knob."

The knob! We had never checked the knob before. What if the door was locked? I couldn't believe I'd forgotten something so simple. After all the planning!

"Open the door!" Bruce barked.

The knob turned easily in my hand. Out through the open door came the musty smell of something that hadn't seen the light of day for a long time. I was suddenly scared. Were we doing the right thing? Months before I'd promised myself that I'd do anything to protect myself from the vampire, and now I was taking my brother to him. We would save Luke in the end, but what if the plan didn't work?

Bruce nodded to the coffin. It was near the back wall, sitting white and steel-like in the corner. There was a large silver clasp at the front, and this bothered me for only an instant because Luke's feet and the sharp pain that met up with my right shin quickly distracted me.

"Ouch!" I wailed into the darkness, and bent to caress my throbbing flesh.

"Shhh!" Bruce commanded, dragging the prisoner to the coffin. At the foot of it they stopped. I followed, my heart beating within me like a hundred firecrackers going off.

"I'll hook him to the wall there," Bruce said. Directly to the right of the coffin was a large nail. It protruded from the dank wall like a finger. "Grab the rope from my pants," Bruce ordered. He had his hands full with Luke.

Walking behind him, I peeked gingerly under Bruce's shirt. Below the bottom edge of his shirt, a piece of rope stuck out. With a grand pull I yanked it free, but not before I heard Bruce yell.

"Crap!"

I tried not to smile as Bruce had me help him tie Luke's hands to the wall. He was sobbing now, my dear brother who I didn't think could cry. And I think he was begging, too.

Did I really care so little about my brother that I would even *pretend* to leave him here to become a vampire? Was I so angry?

"Maybe…" I began, because I knew then what I needed to say to both my brother and the boy I loved with all my heart. Only I was interrupted. The sound began as a quiet tapping on the basement steps leading up to the door—the same door we'd entered only moments before. The sound continued as the door was opened slowly, as the little light left outside crept into the chilly basement of the vampire. Then a voice pierced the darkness.

"So, children, you've been caught by me at last."

# CHAPTER 15

Other than the small light bulb hanging like a dead man from the ceiling, the basement was dark. An eerie glow forced itself through the lone bulb and lit up Mr. Grant's face just enough for me to recognize the monster he was.

He was an old vampire, as decrepit and pale as an old gnarled tree. He had a thick mane of white hair, large brown moles on his hands, and used a cane for support. He hobbled over to us and smiled. An empty hollow mouth greeted me.

Well, at least he won't be able to bite, I thought to myself, at the same time wondering if he'd managed to kill my cat instead of the person I thought had done it. I could almost hear my neck squeaking as I searched for my companions. But I was alone; the others had slipped away and left me there!

"So, you've come to steal from me, have you?"

"Steal?" I gulped, taking two steps backward.

The spotted hand reached out. The warmth of it warmed my flesh. I looked down, fully expecting to see long nails, but in their place were clipped round moons.

"You ought to be afraid," the vampire said, holding my arm. "It's very difficult to save food when hooligans sneak inside your house for whatever they want."

"Hoo—li-gans?" I answered, fully expecting a slithery slide on the neck.

"Come…look." The hand directed me to the white coffin with the metal clasps sitting in the corner of the basement. I was sure it would be fur-lined—red—and that Mr. Grant had some fake fangs in there with which to chew on his victims.

But when I peered down I saw nothing but white packages, vegetables in plastic bags, and a couple of ice-cube trays.

"You can see I have no candy in there," Mr. Grant remarked, pushing my head down just a little to see. The smell of meat wafted through my nostrils like smelly socks, and my eyes blinked once, then twice, at the chill now meeting up with my face.

Mr. Grant released his spotted hand and I was able to stand. But just barely. My legs were shaking so much, and my heart was beating so fast, that, as yet, it hadn't occurred to me that Mr. Grant might not be a vampire after all.

"Would you like anything?" he asked.

With my head bowed I apologized for something I was never planning to do. When I dared look up I saw into his mouth, the tunnel of death, and Mr. Grant escorted me to the basement door.

"In the future, please come to my front door if you're hungry," he said. "I would be happy to share. Oh, I almost forgot. Wait here just a minute."

The beast turned and walked away slowly, *clip-clopping* up the inside stairs leading to his house. And though my heart pounded I didn't move until he'd returned with the casserole dish.

"Thank your mother for me, will you?" he asked, handing me the clean yellow dish. "It was nice of her to think of me."

I nodded, unsure of how to respond. My tongue was as dry as a piece of bark and I had no idea what to do with it.

* * *

June was screaming, "Don't come near me!"

A week had passed since the incident at Mr. Grant's—a week of total loneliness and fear. Only my parents would speak to me. And my teacher at school. Everyone else was as frantic as a deer in the scope of a rifle.

I tried everything. Showing my clean neck. Standing in front of mirrors where you could still see me. Even wearing the cross around my neck that my mother had purchased. But nothing worked.

And now June was screaming like her death was imminent. I'd made the mistake of knocking at her window at 10 P.M. I'd just barely worked things out with Bruce. In the end, his logical thoughts had returned. He'd checked my neck very closely and finally given me the A-OK.

June was another story. But I figured this was because she was a girl and girls got much more emotional than boys. I also figured that church had done something to mess up her brain a bit—because they were always talking about the devil and stuff—but I tried to balance her lack of control with a smile.

"June, look!" I said. "Do you see any fangs?"

June didn't respond. She shut her drapes. After a few minutes she opened them to see me still standing there.

"Mr. Grant isn't a vampire!" I yelled.

Suddenly, another face pressed itself against the window—the shimmering face of Tracey in a floral patterned nightgown that looked more like a prom dress.

"Maybe you should listen," she squeaked.

I nodded, unsure of how June would respond. When the drapes fell back to reveal nothing but fabric my heart sank.

But in a moment I heard a whisper behind me.

"Sam! Where are you?" It was June's voice.

I waved my hands in the dark. I could see June and Tracey, but their eyes had evidently not yet adjusted to see me. Finally, their bare feet traipsed the few steps to the window where I stood. A strange smell of garlic reached my nostrils.

Tracey was the first to speak. "I need to see your teeth closer up," she said. From her pocket she withdrew a flashlight. I opened my mouth and smiled forcefully so that she could see every tooth.

"I think Sam's telling us the truth," she said, brushing her long strands from her face. "I don't think Sam would lie about something like this."

"Unless she was a vampire," June croaked.

Tracey rolled her eyes. "Come and take a closer look," she said, directing the flashlight even closer to my mouth. June took a closer look. After she'd prodded a few of my teeth with her finger, she stepped back.

Seeming satisfied, Tracey directed the flashlight to the lawn. She turned to June. "Well, if Sam's a vampire, she'd surely have some fangs by now."

I nodded, but June wasn't easily convinced. She held up a small mirror directly in front of my face and smashed the glass into my nose. Fortunately, the glass didn't break, although my nose hurt a little. She removed a few pieces of garlic from her pajama pocket and dropped them to the lawn. Finally, she smiled. "I think she's OK," she said.

Tracey smiled. "I bet you were scared," she said.

I nodded, breathing deeply through my mouth. What was there to say now that both of them knew I wasn't a vampire?

"I'd better go," I mumbled finally, but not before Tracey had reached for my arm, making me jump just a little.

"Want to sleep over?" she asked.

I hesitated for only a moment. This was the first time since the baptism that I'd been asked to join them. Should I? And then Luke's possible thoughts of me sunk deep into my flesh, almost like a wicked tattoo, and I knew I needed to return home, though I didn't know what I was going to do after that.

* * *

Luke was ignoring me. I was sitting on his bed, and Joshua was sitting next to me. "I hate you!" he finally said.

I agreed that he should hate me, because for the first time in more than three years I understood the word hate and what it felt like.

"How could you...you...tie me up like that?" he sobbed.

"I don't know," I said weakly. But I did know. I'd hated him for hating Joshua. For liking and then hating him, and then liking and hating him again. He was wishy-washy, like what people used to call an "Indian giver." Here, you can have this. No, I want it back. It made me crazy inside.

Joshua was sobbing. "Sorry, Brother," he said, his stomach bobbing.

Luke looked at Joshua briefly and then back at me. It was if the words meant nothing to him.

"I thought that...Mr. Grant was going to kill me!"

"I'm sorry too." I was looking down at my hands now and not into my brother's eyes. A feeling of warmth suddenly caressed my shoulders and I knew it was Joshua. "You can do it," he seemed to be telling me through his touch.

I wiped at my eyes and forced them to look into the eyes of my brother. When had the change occurred in me? When had I begun to see how afraid he was? My heart searched for an answer to tell him, a truth to relay, a thought to share, but none came. Just a large lump that felt more like a huge peach stone.

How could I have done this to him? How could I have hated him so?

But in the next instant I knew. It was as if a sudden burst of light had suddenly traveled to my brain and was speaking to me in a human voice. It said, "You are angry at everyone because of your father."

For an instant, I didn't let out my breath, but kept it held within me like an old wound. And then it was released and I began to sob.

"I love...you, Brother," I finally said, meaning it this time. And my brother, for the first time that I could remember, looked over at me and said, "I'm sorry too...Sister."

I don't know how long we hugged that night, my two brothers and I. But I will tell you this, and this is the complete truth: I have never felt so happy and complete in my whole life.

# CHAPTER 16

"Tell me about Daddy," I said. Mother was as silent as death and practically just as lifeless. We were sitting in her bedroom on the orange and green bedspread that reminded me of a garden of weeds.

"What do you want to know?" she answered.

I couldn't tell if she was nervous or not, and so I said, "I want to know why you divorced, but I don't want to hear about Daddy forgetting the milk or something else dumb like that."

My mother gave a short little laugh, kind of like a squeaky sprinkler knob. And then she said, "Two people need to get along to live with one another, as you know. And when they don't get along they need to be separated."

"Like you and Daddy, I suppose."

"Yes. Like me and Daddy."

"Sometimes Luke and I hate each other," I said, knowing full well that it was cruel to use Luke's name when we had just made up. I would never forget yesterday, not as long as I lived, but I could still use the pain of it as a way of convincing my mother to talk to me.

"I know," my mother said, surprising me. "I know it's sometimes difficult to get along with your brother. But your relationship…with Luke is very different from that of your father and I."

"How?"

"Well, your father and I were married."

"So what?" I said, knowing I was being rude, but wanting the true answer out.

"When you are married," my mother began, "you have certain duties to each other…"

"Like bringing home the milk when you're asked," I said. I thought this was a good joke, but Mother didn't laugh.

"More than just milk," Mother answered. "When you're older, you'll understand more than I can tell you."

I wondered what that left in terms of secrets, if anything. Mother patted me on the knee.

"Did you ever love Daddy?" I asked, thinking of the way Noah in the Bible had obviously loved his wife to travel in a stinky ark all the way to a new land, and how Mary must have loved God to be the mother of God's son.

Mother was silent, and then she said, "I suppose I did once. All you need to know now is that I love you and your brother. That will never change. And Carl loves you too and wants so much to be your daddy."

Tears welled up in my mother's eyes. I tried not to look at her. There she was, trying to be happy again. Trying to prove to me that life was different since Carl had come along and that she was glad.

The funny thing was, I was beginning to agree with her.

* * *

"Steven's father won't let him out for two weeks!" Bruce said as we walked down to his place.

I would have laughed, but the situation with Mr. Grant was no longer anything but solemn to me. I would never forgive myself for what I'd done. And I was surprised that I'd gotten off so easily with my mother.

After the episode with Luke at Mr. Grant's, I wondered if my mother would ever let me out again. But two days later I was free.

"He didn't do much," I answered. "His father is too strict."

Bruce nodded his head as if he were remembering the incident after the fire caught hold of his neck. The separation had been major even then—almost six months. But of course Bruce had had to heal and stuff.

Still, I was glad for one thing: my mother's punishments never lasted more than a moment in comparison to Steve's.

Suddenly, Bruce stopped and shifted his jeans like he had ants in his pants. I started to giggle. Bruce glared at me. "Stop it!" he said.

"Sorry," I answered, but I didn't mean it. He looked so funny!

"Got ants crawling around in your pants?" I asked.

Bruce was still. He looked down at the road. "No," he said.

"Sure looks like it," I answered, looking down at his butt. "Maybe they're out now," I said, because he'd stopped wiggling. I wondered if the problem was his underwear creeping up but didn't say anything.

Bruce turned away from me and walked toward my house, even though we were going over to his. His tennis shoes plopped against the sidewalk like a long belly that reached to the ground. Bruce was still fidgeting with his pant leg and I wondered what was really bothering him.

Perhaps I shouldn't have laughed. Maybe Luke was right. Maybe I was as mean as I made everyone else out to be.

When I got up to Bruce he was already rounding the corner.

"Where ya going?" I asked.

"None of your business," he answered, not even looking at me.

It was beginning to get hot. At the beginning of April a cool breeze should have tossed my hair and caused the hairs to prickle on my arms, but it wasn't breezy today. Six weeks from now, school would be out, and the spring weather that felt like summer now would become the real thing. After summer I would be returning to school—to sixth grade. I was scared spitless, but I didn't have to think about that now. So why was I?

Bruce had almost reached June's before I realized where he was going. She was sitting out front as if expecting him, taking shade under the large oak tree out front. She smiled when she saw us and then quickly frowned.

Bruce sat down slowly at her feet as if he were suddenly an old man with arthritis—like Mr. Grant without the cane. I joined him but sat nearer June. "I'm not going to talk until *she* goes," he said.

June looked at Bruce like the new therapist she was becoming. "Why don't you want to see Sam?" she asked.

"Because she's stupid," Bruce said.

I might have laughed if not for the fact that I knew Bruce was serious. I had really hurt him somehow and I wasn't sure what to do about it.

"Is that correct?" June asked, turning to me with thoughtful eyes.

"I guess," I answered, put on the spot, but not knowing how to get out of it.

"I'm not going to say anything until she goes," Bruce said.

"How do you feel about that, Sam?" June asked.

I stood. I was angry now. I had no idea why Bruce was mad at me. I'd teased him before. Lots of times. Why was he so angry all of a sudden? I turned from the staring twosome who suddenly felt like a group of ninth-graders parading around my soul. Without looking back even once I walked away, clear up the street, and rounded the corner home. Only I didn't go to my house.

* * *

I was in the swing, high in flight, when I spotted Tracey nearby at the slides. I watched her for a moment in her perfect hair and clothes and thought again about her baptism a few days before. A little boy was climbing up the back of the slide and she was catching him at the other end. His high squeals sent chills up my arms and reminded me of how things used to be when my daddy still lived with us and my brother could spend more time with me and my mother seemed to care. Why couldn't I erase those memories?

The feeling at Tracey's baptism was unlike any feeling I'd ever experienced before, other than when I was reading the Bible. I'd felt the warmth a couple of times since then: when June shared that she knew the Mormon church was true, and when I'd forgiven my brothers. The feeling had been a warmth that seemed to travel up my back and land in my heart.

Only it didn't stay. If it had, I might not have dragged my brother Luke to Mr. Grant's house so I could scare him. Perhaps I would have never yelled at Carl or told Luke that Joshua was a whale. Maybe I would have been kinder to everyone, including my mother. And maybe, just maybe, I would have forgiven myself by now.

When I looked up, Tracey was coming my way. She held the tiny hand of a boy with short brown hair and gleaming green eyes.

The boy was the first one to speak. "Hi," he said. I figured he was probably three or four years old because his backside was too flat to be covered by a diaper and he could stand pretty securely on the ground without toppling over.

"Hi!" Tracey echoed. "What are you doing here?"

I was suddenly thinking of Tracey's baptism and the way her hair looked, all sticky flat to her face as she came out of the water, her clothes clinging to her like a vampire to someone's neck.

She smiled. Her teeth were perfect, just like everything else she was wearing. She wore a striped orange shirt with a collar, a choker of stars, and flared jeans covering, I was sure, more than perfect shoes.

"Are you having fun?" I asked the little boy so I could avoid Tracey's question.

"His name is Todd," she said.

"Hi, Todd," I said.

He smiled a toothy grin. "Hi, girl with short hair," he said.

Tracey laughed. "Her name is Samantha," she said.

"Sam, to you," I said.

"Sam you...Sam you...Sam you..."

I was suddenly smiling. "I like to swing," I finally said, but feeling pretty stupid at the same time.

"Me too," Tracey offered, surprising me by walking over to the swing next to mine and sitting down. "Sometimes I come here to think," she said.

"Me too!"

Tracey giggled. And then she became somewhat solemn. "Right before I was baptized was my favorite time."

"Oh," I answered, not knowing what else to say.

"Of course I was by myself." She looked down at Todd, who was playing with a bug he'd found in the grass. "I couldn't have brought anyone then."

"Why not?" I asked.

"I have many brothers and sisters. Noisy. I needed somewhere quiet. Everyone goes to the park but hardly anyone comes to the school when they don't have to."

I agreed with her, thinking about all of the times I'd come here for that very reason.

"What do you think about?" I asked her boldly, because for some reason I wanted to know. Maybe I thought if I let her talk she would answer the question in my mind about 1 Nephi 3:7, or maybe I just wanted someone to talk to that day. Maybe I needed to feel that feeling again, and perhaps she would be the one to give it to me. But I knew this: I needed to ask.

"Do you really want to know?" she countered, twisting her left braid with her pinky finger. "I mean, I thought you hated me."

I'm sure I blushed. This girl could see right through me. "I guess I did once," I told her truthfully. "June was my very best friend, you know."

Tracey nodded. "She talks about you all the time."

"She does?"

Tracey looked away from my eyes and up to the mountains.

"Have you ever been up there?" she asked.

"Sure. Lots of times."

"We go up there every summer. It's so much fun."

"Ever been to Bear Lake?"

"No."

"It's a great place," I said. "Maybe some time you can come with us."

"Without your dad?"

The question struck me as funny. I didn't know what to say. It was as if she knew he hadn't come the last time either.

Tracey shifted in her seat. "I mean, your real dad. He doesn't come to see you anymore, does he?"

"No."

"I can't believe it. If my dad ever left me like that I think I would die...sorry. I mean..."

"That's OK. I don't know where he is, if you really want to know."

"Sorry," Tracey said again, looking down at her feet. "You probably think I'm a mean person."

"No," I said, although I'd obviously felt that way before. But not now. Something in Tracey's manner made me feel sorry for having hated her. It was as if I suddenly saw in her a part of me—the part of myself that I'd lost.

I decided to change the subject. "So what kind of stuff do you think about when you come here?"

"Well...right before I was going to get baptized I thought a lot about how scary it was going to be going under the water."

"Was it?" I asked.

"For a second," she answered. "But the water was warm and I could hear the groggling sound of the water going through my ears."

I laughed. "What's groggling?"

"You know, kind of like air bubbles."

I knew what that was like. I'd been swimming in Bear Lake lots of times.

"Well," she continued, "I also thought about what it would feel like to get the Holy Ghost."

"Is he full of holes?" I asked, and then suddenly felt stupid. The "holy" Tracey probably meant was the holy spirit of God.

"Of course not," Tracey answered, looking down at her brother briefly.

"In some of the discussions they told me that I would feel the Holy Ghost, but that he wouldn't be able to be with me all of the time because I wasn't baptized."

A faint glow traveled up my back. "What are discussions?" I asked.

"Oh, they're kind of like...talks. You know, some missionaries come to your house and they teach you about Jesus Christ."

"What are missionaries?" I asked. I had heard the word missionaries but couldn't imagine missionaries here when they were supposed to be in Africa with all of the people who didn't know about God.

"You've probably seen them," Tracey answered. "They wear black suits and white shirts and ride bikes."

I nodded my head yes. Actually, I remembered seeing someone like that just a few days ago at Mr. Grant's.

"Do they hold up a book?" I asked.

Tracey seemed confused. For a moment she seemed to be going inside her brain to try to figure out my question. Finally, she smiled, and said, "If you mean the Book of Mormon, yes, the missionaries hold up that book and tell you about some of the things that are in it. Of course, you are expected to read the whole thing."

"How many pages does it have?" I asked.

Tracey was reflective. "Oh, I don't know, but it's sort of long and some of the words are hard to understand."

"Then why read it." It wasn't a question, but suddenly Tracey was looking into my blue eyes and they seemed to be telling me something:

You need to listen now...

A warm feeling, just the same as a few moments before, spread up my back and into my heart. "What's the book about?" I asked.

"Well, it's about Indians…"

"You mean, cowboys and Indians?" I had a sudden thought of Joshua with his shirt off.

Tracey shrugged. "All I know is that it's about Nephites and Indians, except for in this book they are called Lamanites."

"Lemon whats?"

"Lam-an-ites."

"Lamnites!"

Todd giggled. Standing up and walking over to his sister, he said, "I want to swing!"

"See what I mean?" Tracey sighed, picking up her brother and placing him in the swing she had been sitting in.

"Push him to me and I'll tease him by trying to grab his legs," I said.

Tracey smiled and pushed her brother just a little.

"Go! Go!" he said, as I tried to catch his small feet.

He was pushed slightly higher, and as I tried to catch his feet, I thought about what Tracey had said about the Mormon church and I wondered if she would know the answer to 1 Nephi 3:7.

# CHAPTER 17

"Where have you been, young lady?" It was past eight o'clock, and my mother probably thought I was going to turn into the great pumpkin or something, because she was shaking.

"At the school," I answered.

"Do you have any idea what time it is?"

"Eight o'clock," I answered, even though I knew it was way past eight.

"It's almost nine, for your information."

Well, I didn't care about her information, so I just stared into her bulging brown eyes.

"June was here. I had no idea what to tell her."

"Sorry," I said. The feeling of warmth was gone again.

"Next time, tell me where you're going, OK?"

"OK," I answered blandly. I wasn't two years old, after all. Why should she care?

Carl came around the corner. "All the dinner's gone. If you'd been here you would have had something to eat."

"Yeah," Joshua said, peeking around the couch and into the kitchen.

"Yeah," Luke echoed, peeking next to him.

"You guys are pigs!" I said, but then I smiled just a little and gave them a wink.

"Samantha!" said Carl.

"What?" I asked.

"As for your rude language, I'm getting pretty sick and tired of hearing it."

"I was only…"

"Apologize to your brothers."

"I won't!"

"You will!"

"Mother?!"

"Apologize to your brothers."

"Sorry, Josh. Sorry, Luke."

"That's OK, Sis," Joshua answered, giving me a wink.

"Yeah, OK," Luke muttered, turning back to the television program.

"Now, don't you feel better?" Carl asked.

I turned away from him. "I guess," I said. "Can I go to my room now?"

Mother gave me a slight hug, as if my shoulders were the only part of my body that needed hugging, and Carl patted me lightly on the back as I passed by. Joshua and Luke merely stuck out their tongues like garter snakes.

* * *

"Bruce thinks you're rude," June said. We were sitting in the trailer house, and fortunately June hadn't asked about hypnotizing me.

"Why?" I asked.

"You know why. I promised him that I wouldn't tell anyone but I think you should know."

"What?"

"That night when we took your brother Luke to Mr. Grant's, well, he was punished pretty bad for doing that. His father doesn't want you hanging around him any more."

"Oh," I said, hardly believing her words, but believing them at the same time. "How was he punished?"

"You've got to promise not to tell," June said, eyeing me closely for honesty.

I pushed my body against the wall of the trailer and adjusted the pillow behind me. "Shoot," I said.

"You promise?"

"I promise."

"His dad took a wooden spoon to him."

I thought for a moment about what June could possibly mean. I ate with a spoon for breakfast. Spoons were used for soup, too, and for digging in the dirt—although I hadn't done much of that lately, though I still kept the silver spoon that Luke had given me by my bedside. "It was a large one his mother had hanging on the wall for decoration."

"Do you mean his daddy hit him with it?" I asked, surprised.

"Of course, dummy. Bruce says he was pounded on the backside at least ten times. He lost count after six."

No wonder he was mad...and sore. "I need to tell him how sorry I am." I stood, wishing to exit, but June restrained me with her hand. "Now, you don't want me to break your other pinky," she said.

I looked down at my hand. My little finger was still crooked, and would forever be because of June.

"You said it was an accident," I said.

"Well, yes, the first time it was," June answered.

I hid my hand underneath the other one as if in hiding it I would be protected. But suddenly the camper door swung open with a loud *creak!* An angry face peered inside.

"I thought I'd find you two in here!" the voice raged.

I didn't even have to look to know that the angry voice belonged to June's father. I hadn't seen or talked with him in months, but I suddenly remembered Bruce's comments about him: "He got mad at me for being inside his trailer."

"Didn't I tell you to stay out of here, and away from that girl?"

He said, "that girl" as if I were the poison that had killed my cat.

"Yes, but..."

"But nothing! You! Out!"

"Dad! It isn't fair! I like Sam. She is..."

I stood, and without even a look back at June, I raced from the trailer's interior.

* * *

"I've lost my best friend. Her daddy...hates me and I don't even know why," I said.

Joshua and Luke were sitting together on Luke's bed. "It's not you," Luke said. "It's June's mother."

"June's mother?" What could an *empty* trailer have to do with June's mother?

"I heard them talking once," Joshua said. "June and Tracey. Something about June's mother using the trailer as a hideaway whenever she got mad at June's father. Some kind of memory thing."

"Are you sure?"

"Sure, I'm sure. I would watch myself in there if I were you. Maybe you should avoid the place altogether."

I nodded. "Bruce hates me too, you know," I said, as if telling them about June wasn't enough for me to feel peace within myself.

"It isn't you," Joshua broke in.

"How would you know?"

"Bruce talked to me yesterday. Said his dad was pretty mad about him going to Mr. Grant's like that."

"I don't know what to do. I think I'm gonna die," I said.

"You won't," Joshua countered.

When I looked up, Joshua was messing with the sheet as if he were uncomfortable with something. And then he continued, "I haven't always been liked. Being alone is hard."

I believed him and said so. Luke reached over and punched Joshua on the arm.

"Thanks," Joshua said, as if the punch of friendship meant more than any of my words.

"Maybe you should get another boyfriend," offered Joshua.

I was momentarily surprised. How did they know?

"Like you, for example?" I said. It was supposed to be a joke but neither Luke nor Joshua laughed.

"I'm kidding," I said.

"No, you're not," Joshua said. "Even if you weren't my stepsister you would never want me for a boyfriend."

I didn't know what to say. Instead, I looked over at Luke. "What should I do?" I asked.

"Get another friend if you want," Luke said.

"Everyone hates me," I said.

"No, they don't," Joshua answered, patting me lightly on the arm. "We like you. Right, Luke?"

Luke looked into my eyes and winked. "You're my sister. I gotta like you."

"Yeah, just like Mother and Carl and...Daddy," I said, turning away and looking out the window for comfort. But there was none. None at all.

# CHAPTER 18

October began with a whirl of leaves and myriad papers blown from too-lightly sealed garbage cans. The muck stuck in window wells and between doors and walls. In less than a month, Halloween would be here and I would be trick-or-treating alone—if I did it at all.

Though I'd begun the summer alone, I'd ended it spending most of the summer with Tracey and June, learning to apply makeup and wearing cool clothes so that the boys would notice us. Tracey had even shared with me her testimony of the church, and we'd discussed some of the stories she had read in the Book of Mormon. But I hadn't asked her the question that was plaguing my heart.

I didn't go to June's anymore. She'd come to my house or we'd go to Tracey's. June figured it would be safer, and I agreed with her.

Today, Mr. Green was outside of his house gathering the last of the summer supplies and trimming his plants to prepare them for winter. He looked up and waved when he saw me. I'd been afraid to talk to Mr. Green ever since June's revelation that he was her psychiatrist.

But now there was no escaping him.

"Hello," I said, walking up to the fence and peeking in.

"Open the gate and come inside," Mr. Green requested, standing up from the cold ground and waving me over.

I flipped up the metal latch and walked inside, shutting the gate behind me. When I reached Mr. Green he was already in the backyard in one of the painted chairs.

"Sit," he said.

"I don't want to be figured out," I said, wiping off a few stray leaves and sitting in the cold seat.

Mr. Green smiled and slicked back his thick white hair. "So, you've talked to June," he said.

"Yes. I had no idea. If I did…"

"I hope you still like me," he offered.

I looked into his penetrating blue eyes and nodded a yes. Even knowing the secret I still thought him to be a kind old man. Just not near as kind as I'd first thought.

When I didn't answer he said, "Well, I suppose that doesn't matter. How are you doing?"

"Fine," I lied.

"And your family?"

"Fine, too," I answered.

"How are you getting along with your brothers?"

"They're OK, I guess."

"You guess? I think it a fine thing to have brothers. I never had them myself, you know."

"No, I didn't know." For a second or two I thought about what I would ask him. And then it came to me. It was a dumb question but the only question I could think of. "Is your dog, Charlie, still buried back there?" I pointed to the spot that last year had held a mound of dirt the size of his dog. It was flat now and there were many weeds growing where the empty spot had been.

"Charlie's still there," Mr. Green answered. "I hope."

A strange chill raced across my back, and then I asked, "You loved him a lot, didn't you?"

Mr. Green hesitated. "He was the only dog I had."

I didn't know what to say after that, and we were both silent, breathing in the afternoon air. Finally Mr. Green said something that really made me think. It was as if he knew. It was as if he could see into my soul or something. There was no judgment in his eyes, only love. But the question penetrated my soul like a spear.

"You're not happy, are you, Samantha?"

I couldn't believe he'd figured it out. That he could see the blackness of my pain, my sad and lonely heart. Could he also see my anger? The terrible thing I had done to Luke and Bruce? The misunderstandings I'd had with my mother? The secrets it was hurting me not to know?

When I was silent he placed his weathered hands on mine. "I understand." And then he stood. "Come with me," he said.

I followed him into the old house, like a little soldier. I'd never been invited into Mr. Green's house before, and part of me was excited at the prospect. The side screen opened with a *creee-eeak* and the solid wooden door was pushed open. Mr. Green stood within what I imagined was the living room, but there was no couch and no television.

Old wooden chairs stood in various corners, overshadowed by a large bookshelf that reached clear up to the ceiling. The floor was simply wood; I could see no carpet at all.

"Wow!" I said, looking up.

"I'm glad you approve," Mr. Green said, walking to the bookshelf and retrieving a blue book. He waved me over.

"I've been waiting quite a few years to give this to just the right person."

"Oh," I said, hardly believing that I could be the person Mr. Green was waiting for.

"This is a special book. It has marvelous answers to many questions." He touched the cover lovingly with his hand, brushing the blueness of the book as if it were his dog, Charlie.

"When I lost my wife...I found this book."

"What's it called?" I asked, suddenly too curious to wait for the story of Mr. Green's past.

Mr. Green sat on the chair nearest him. "That chair behind you," he said. "Bring it yonder."

"Where?" I asked.

"Over by me. I want to show you the book."

I was afraid the chair would break when I lifted it, but it was heavy and seemed sturdy enough to hold my small body, especially when Mr. Green's was much larger and his chair was holding him just fine.

I sat the chair across from him, thinking it the best place, but Mr. Green directed me over beside him. "I won't bite," was all he said, making me think, however briefly, about my unsolved problems with Mr. Grant, the used-to-be vampire.

Mr. Green's hand was still placed warmly over the blue book. Finally, when he could see that I was ready, I guess, he removed his hand. A golden man was on the front cover and he was blowing some kind of horn. Below him I could read the words on the face of the cover: "The Book of Mormon."

I couldn't breathe. I knew that name. But Mr. Green had opened the front flap. He was pointing to some handwritten words inside the cover.

"Read them," he directed.

"To Charles: I know that the Lord lives, that our Father in Heaven loves each of his children. I know that the church is true. I have known it for many years. Please read the book. Receive of its goodness. Come unto the Lord through baptism. I will always love you." The note was signed "Flora."

"Why would Flora want to give a book to your dog?" I asked.

Mr. Green chuckled. "Well," he said, after he'd regained his voice, "my name is Charles. Before Flora and I were married, she had a dog named Charlie. We always laughed about that. It was as if she knew she was going to marry me."

"Do you think she did?" I asked. "I mean, do you think she knew you were the right one?"

"Oh, Samantha, you do ask the questions. Let me see…" He tapped his fingers lovingly on the book. "When Flora met me I was not a member of the church."

"You mean a Mormon," I said.

Mr. Green seemed surprised. "Yes," he said. "I wasn't a Mormon. In fact, I didn't go to any church. I preferred the mountains."

"I like Bear Lake," I said.

"I haven't been there. But I hear it's beautiful."

I smiled.

Mr. Green looked at me tenderly. "Did you go there with your family?" he asked.

I nodded. "The last time I brought June with me."

"And your father?"

"He didn't come."

"I see. You miss your father, don't you?"

"Yes."

"I miss Flora, too. She was the jewel in my crown."

"You have a crown?" I asked.

Mr. Green smiled. "Oh, no, not a real crown. A heavenly crown."

"How can you have a heavenly crown if you're not dead yet?" I asked. "Sorry," I added, "that probably sounded rude."

Mr. Green shut the book. He handed it to me. "The crown is in here," he said, pointing to the book.

How could a crown be mixed in with a bunch of difficult words? But I thanked him anyway. He was old, after all, even if he was a psychiatrist. "Is it golden?" I asked, feeling stupid even as I said it.

"In words, yes."

Golden words…

# CHAPTER 19

The words were there in black and white, and hardly golden, but they did make me think a little.

"And it came to pass that I, Nephi, said unto my father: I will go and do the things which the Lord hath commanded, for I know that the Lord giveth no commandments unto the children of men, save he shall prepare a way for them that they may accomplish the thing which he commandeth them" (1 Nephi 3:7).

It hadn't taken me long to find the mysterious scripture printed on the back of Tracey's baptism invitation. Close to the front of the book, I quickly discovered a list of the chapters, arranged in a similar way to the books of the Bible, with an index and page numbers to help you find the chapter you were looking for.

I wondered who Nephi's father was, so I looked back to the beginning of chapter 3 and found these words in its heading: "Lehi's sons return to Jerusalem to obtain the brass plates…"

So, his name was Lehi.

For a moment I thought of Daddy. Three years had passed since he'd left us, and I was living my life without him. Now I was going about my life as if he'd *almost* never existed. Where was he?

If only I had a daddy like Nephi had. One who would talk to me and who I could tell things to, like Nephi was able to do. I didn't know a lot about the commandments, but Mother had taught me about the golden rule: "Do unto others as you would have them do unto you."

I decided to read the book. It couldn't hurt me to try anyway. But my eyes were tired. I laid the blue book with the golden man on my bedside table and turned out the light.

\* \* \*

It was Halloween, but the snow covered the ground early this year, and children of all sizes and costumes were coming to the door in heavy winter coats. One little guy was even wearing boots. I had decided not to dress up or go out.

"I's a snowman," he said, turning for me to see the backside of his costume, which was just about as interesting as the front. He wore a long white coat of fur, probably his mother's, and his tiny nose was painted orange. When he smiled, the painted round balls that served as rocks for his mouth shifted and thinned into a black lake. I tried not to laugh.

I held out the bucket. "You can have two," I said, even though Mother had given me strict instructions to give out only one to each trick-or-treater.

Toward the end of the night, near nine o'clock, the stream of trick-or-treaters had all but halted. A few tall ones came occasionally, and each time, although I hated to admit it, I wished to see Bruce's and June's faces. But they never came.

I did see Tracey, though. She was dressed as a ghost, all in white and silver. "How come you're not out trick-or-treating?" she asked.

"Mother needed me at home this year," I lied.

"Oh," she answered, looking past me into the living room.

"Why aren't you with June?" I asked.

The ghost shrugged her shoulders. "She decided to go with Bruce, I guess. Want to come with me?"

"No," I said, feeling honest about it this time.

"All you need is a sheet."

"With holes," I answered uneasily.

Tracey smiled at me, and I could almost see the thought that came over her—the question I had asked her about the Holy Ghost.

"Are you sure you don't want to come?" she asked.

"Sure, I'm sure. But you could come in if you want."

"Really?"

Tracey seemed momentarily surprised, as if she'd just won an award, and then without another word she stepped into the kitchen.

\* \* \*

I opened the blue book and began to read: "I Nephi, having been born of goodly parents, therefore I was taught somewhat in all the learning of my father…" (1 Nephi 1:1).

I was about to skip to 1 Nephi 3:7 for a moment, but the word "goodly" jumped before my eyes like a basketball. Was there really such a thing as a good parent? The word made me suddenly uneasy. Maybe this book wasn't right for me after all.

I was about to close it, leaving it to some future ruin, when a voice spoke.

"What-cha doin'?" it asked.

Joshua stood in front of me. He was wearing a red striped shirt, and it was untucked, revealing a puffy section of his belly. I looked down at it, trying to move the piece of fabric with my eyes.

He smiled and tucked the flap in. "What-cha reading?" he asked.

"Just a book," I answered lamely.

"What's it about?" he asked.

"You don't want to know."

He sat on the edge of the bed. "Why, is it scary?" he asked.

I thought for a moment. "Sort of," I answered.

"I don't like scary books either," he said. "So who's the gold guy? The serial killer?"

"I don't think so," I said. "He's probably an angel." The thought that the golden man was an angel had first occurred to me as I had placed the book on my end table. The angel was blowing a horn to wake people up or something, but I couldn't be sure.

"The Book of Mormon," Joshua read slowly, looking down at me. "I think I've heard of that."

I couldn't believe that Joshua had ever heard of it. "When?" I asked.

"My mom…well, she showed it to me once…I think…in the bookstore. Where'd you get yours?"

"Mr. Green," I answered.

"A nice man. So why is it scary?"

I wondered if I should tell him. Would he think I was nuts? The wall had all but dissolved now between Joshua and me. Would I create an even thicker one by sharing what was in my heart?

# CHAPTER 20

"I don't know what a goodly parent is," I said, showing Joshua the verse in 1 Nephi 1:1.

"Well, you know: a parent who is nice and teaches you stuff."

"I mean…oh, I don't know."

Joshua was thoughtful. He was looking down at his shoes, I guess to see if they could give him the answer. After a few minutes he looked up at me. "I think it means that this guy's parents—what was his name? Nephi?"

I nodded.

"Well, this Nephi had good parents who taught him stuff."

"Mother doesn't talk to me like I wish she would," I said.

"My mother did."

"Good for you," I said.

Joshua scuffed his shoe back and forth across the green carpet. "Sorry," he said. "I just meant that I had a good mother."

"Your mother killed herself," I said, knowing I sounded rude, but also knowing that there wasn't a good mother out there.

Joshua was quiet. "I thought you wanted me to help," he said.

I shrugged my shoulders and looked away from his twisting hands. It was like Joshua was nervous or something, and then I felt ashamed. "I shouldn't have said that about your mother."

"She really was a good one," Joshua said, placing his hands on his pant legs and wiping off something I couldn't see. "She was happy, too. I remember once I came in crying because I'd fallen off my bike. She looked at me real nice and said, 'Joshie, let me fix you up.' And you know, she did."

I thought it strange that Joshua's mother could fix her son up but commit suicide herself, but I didn't say anything to Joshua.

"She called you Joshie?"

Joshua laughed. "It was my nickname."

"Your father doesn't call you that."

"Father wouldn't. He's too serious."

I laughed at that, a connection between us healing old wounds.

"You know, I think your mother is nice too."

I smiled over at him.

"Last year, when I ate all that candy…" he paused for a moment and looked deeply into my eyes for understanding, "…your mother cared that I was all right."

All I could remember was the scolding he'd received. Had my mother actually been nice to Joshua?

"She tucks me in bed just like Luke, you know. And she fixes me meals, and when I ask for seconds she doesn't tell me that I'm too fat to have a second plate."

"I didn't notice," I said.

"She does stuff for you, too," Joshua added.

I couldn't believe he was bringing me into the picture. My mother had sometimes talked to me, but only a little—she had hardly been a good mother like Joshua was suggesting. And now her new son was going to tell me about all of her goodness?

I shrugged Joshua away. "Maybe you'd better go now," I said.

But Joshua wouldn't be put off. "Yesterday I heard her talking to my father," he said.

"You must have heard it from the bedroom," I said, thinking he was finally going to change the subject.

Joshua nodded. "How did you know?"

"That's the only way to find out anything," I said. "So what did you hear?"

"Your father's in town," Joshua said. "And your mother is trying to set up a meeting with you and him."

I was stunned.

"He will be getting out next week."

"Getting out?"

"I wasn't sure about that part."

My heart was thundering. "You've got to remember," I said, tugging Joshua's striped shirtsleeve. "Getting out of where?"

Joshua stood, his heavy shoes clumping against the carpet. He walked to the window. "I might be wrong," he said, "but I think I heard that..." Joshua seemed to fumble at the words, and his voice was suddenly silent. "I don't know...if I can say it."

"Say it! Say it!"

Joshua turned. "Your mother really loves you," he said.

My eyes were probably bugging out by then, but I didn't care.

"She wouldn't have kept the secret if she didn't love you."

"What secret?" I was standing now, shaking my fists at him.

"Your father...Oh, Sam, I can hardly say it. Your father was in prison."

# CHAPTER 21

I didn't know what to do. For the first time in my life, the school ground swings had no effect other than causing a headache. My heart was bruised, my thoughts like those of Dorothy in *The Wizard of Oz* when she discovers she no longer has a home.

I was alone. Even Joshua's pestering did little to change my mind.

Everyone was in bed. My mother. Carl. Luke. Even Joshua, although I wasn't sure he was sleeping.

On the ground, next to my feet, sat my pillowcase. And within the pillowcase nestled my clothing, my toothbrush, a little food, two dollars in cash, our only flashlight, and the blue book with the golden angel.

I wasn't sure where to go, but I knew it would have to be far. My first thought after hearing the news of Daddy was to go to him and tell him how sorry I was. But I was too angry, and I knew Daddy didn't need anger since it was probably something like anger that had gotten him into trouble.

What had he done? Killed someone? My heart stopped as I thought about all of my accusations against Mr. String, the cat killer, and Mr. Grant, the vampire. Might Daddy have actually murdered Mr. Green's wife?

It wasn't possible. But what else could it be?

I knew then I should have watched the news, kept up with the "goings-on," as Mother would have said. Perhaps then I would have known what had happened to my father instead of having to hear it from the lips of Joshua.

It was cold, and in my hastiness I'd forgotten to pack a coat. Could I slip back inside my house without getting caught?

No. I'd just have to travel without one.

Stopping the swing, I grabbed for the pillowcase, throwing my baggage over my shoulder like a miniature Santa Claus. Well, there would be no Christmas for me this year. No Thanksgiving. No outing with Carl...

It seemed funny that I would think about my unhappy holidays at a time like this. But it wasn't until I left the schoolyard that I realized why.

* * *

Bruce was leaning out his bedroom window on the second floor. "You're going to do what?" he wailed, making me shiver even more.

"I need a sweater," I said.

In a flash, the window was empty and a light breeze wafted the curtains.

A few minutes passed, minutes that seemed like an eternity. Finally Bruce was standing in front of me with a flashlight.

"Where's the sweater?" I asked.

"Didn't bring it," he answered bluntly.

"I need it."

"I know. I'm not letting you go anywhere."

"I'll just get the sweater at June's," I said. "Or hide out in her trailer until tomorrow afternoon. It'll be a little warmer then." Even as I said it, a cold chill ran up my spine. That was the last place I wanted to be.

"I don't care," Bruce said. "You're not leaving because of me, are you?"

I had to tell him that honestly I hadn't even thought about it, but Bruce didn't believe me. "It's my fault," he said. "It was my idea to go to Mr. Grant's."

I knew it wasn't his idea but I didn't say anything.

"I'm not leaving because of Mr. Grant," I said.

"Why then? Are you still mad at June?"

It was getting very cold. My shoulders were shaking like a horrible earthquake but I was determined to get the sweater and continue on.

"I don't care if it doesn't fit," I said. "A coat would be even better," I added, grasping my thin arms with my cold hands.

113

"You won't want to wear it," Bruce said. "It has a furry collar that looks like a puffball."

"I don't care," I said.

"Just a minute."

I stood in the blistering cold and waited, thinking that I might have been smarter to stop by June's. She might have tried to hypnotize me. And that might have made this journey easier. Why hadn't I thought of her first?

When Bruce returned, he had a brown coat draped over his arm. The long coat had a tan collar that looked like a dead cat. I put it on. The arms fell past my hands and the bottom of the coat touched the grass.

Bruce laughed. "You don't look like my mother," he said.

I didn't laugh back. Well, at least I was warm now. The change in temperature was unmistakable.

"Where are you going?" Bruce asked, as I warmed myself underneath the heavy wool.

"I don't know yet."

"You're lying."

I didn't want to talk to Bruce about lying. I'd had enough lying to last me a century, and way past the time I would be put in my grave.

"Thanks for the coat." I turned, my heart suddenly beating within me. A kiss would have been nice at a time like this. I'd seen it in many romantic movies where the boy or girl had to leave the other for a very long time. But I knew it was a dream. A lie. And so I didn't ask Bruce the question bursting within my heart. I left him standing at the front of his house in the cold without even a jacket.

# CHAPTER 22

Don't ask me why, but on my way to the bus stop I stopped at June's. I was almost past her house when I saw the gentle fluttering of the drapes inside her father's trailer. I didn't know what time it was, but it had to have been well past midnight. Why was June inside her father's trailer so late at night?

I needed to signal her…somehow…without going in.

Perhaps her father had finally allowed her to sleep in there. I flashed my flashlight at the window. Once…twice…three times. On the fourth try a man peeked out.

"Who's out there?" June's father hollered, making my knees feel weak.

I'd already walked a few paces to the trailer by then, but now I was dashing for the street. I'd never been a very fast runner, but that night I ran with the speed of a roadrunner. For an instant I thought of the blue book with the angel on it. I'd read about Nephi and his people crossing the great waters only yesterday. I'd read way past 1 Nephi 3:7 about doing what the Lord commanded. But today, Nephi's heaven-sent direction meant little to me. I just had to get out of there.

Around the corner from June's there was a high wall, and behind the wall a few stores and a small restaurant that was always changing owners. Maybe I could hide there.

Without another thought, I allowed my legs to carry me toward safety, the wool coat dragging behind me like a heavy tail slowing me down. I was almost to the back of the restaurant when the worst possible thing happened. I tripped!

In seconds, I was being dragged to my feet. It was then I realized I still held the flashlight clenched within my right hand. And even worse, the light was still on.

* * *

June's father was pacing the living room in a stumbling fashion, and his eyes looked glazed. Was June's daddy drunk? I had read enough of the Book of Mormon to know it was wrong to get drunk. Why else would Laman and Lemuel get into so much trouble for being drunk on the ship?

I shrugged the thought aside and looked at a corner of the living room. There hung a lamp that looked like a bunch of grapes. It was gold in color and resembled something the angel on the blue book might have carried in case he got hungry.

Under the grapes lamp was a chair of the same color. And next to the chair, a television set with pictures on top. One of them was of June. Another was of a woman with bright red hair and a warm smile. I was sitting on the golden couch across from the television set, feeling like I was on a cop show during the interrogation scene.

"What were you doing?" June's father asked.

"I…"

"Your mother must be worried sick. What were you doing out there in the dark?"

I wanted to ask June's father what he could possibly have been doing inside the trailer late at night, but my voice wouldn't work. Besides, I was pretty sure he'd been drinking.

"All right, Samantha, I'm going to call your mother."

I was silent, trying to work through my thoughts, but never coming to the end of them. If he called my mother I'd have to go home. My mother would ground me again, but that was the least of my worries. I would finally see my father…my father…

* * *

"What were you thinking?" Carl asked. He was pointing his finger at me like my mother always did. His brown hair was a messy wad, and I could see new growth on his chin. He was still wearing his pajamas, as were my mother and brothers, who stood eyeing me from their bedroom.

My mother was sitting on the green chair opposite me. She was crying.

I looked up at Carl, trying to remember why I was leaving. "I'm sorry," I finally said.

"Well, Samantha, sorry won't work this time. Stand up!"

I stood. If I wasn't going to be grounded, what else was there? And then, instinctively, I remembered.

From behind Carl's back, he brought forth a long wooden spoon. "Lean over the couch," he ordered.

"No, Carl! No!" I looked at my mother, who was running over to Carl. An arm was wrapped around his waist.

Carl shrugged her off. "It's about time this little girl learned some manners!" he yelled.

"But not like this, Carl, please!"

"Lean over the couch!"

"Please...Daddy..."

Carl smiled slightly. "Lean over the couch. This will be over in a minute."

I leaned over the couch, sobbing now. What could I do? What could I say? "Please, Carl..." I sobbed. "I was...was afraid of him."

"Afraid of who?" I sensed that he was raising the spoon above me in the air.

"Daddy," I said.

"Your father..." He breathed heavily, as if he hated even the sound of the word.

"I didn't know he was in jail. What if he kills me, too?"

"Kills you? Why would he..."

Suddenly it was if the room and everyone in it were frozen solid. Carl didn't move. The spoon was ready to hit me, and my mother was sobbing close by. I could even smell the scent of chocolate in the room and wondered if Joshua had forgotten his promise.

"Sit down," Carl finally said.

I opened my eyes and raised my thin body to a straightened position. When I looked into Carl's eyes, he was crying. "I'm sorry," he offered.

My mother placed her hand around my arm. "Sit," she said.

# CHAPTER 23

Mother was caressing my wet cheeks. By that time, almost 2 A.M., Joshua and Luke were sitting in the family room with us. My brothers were sitting on the floor, and Carl was sitting across from me on a chair he'd pulled from the corner.

In one month it would be Thanksgiving, a time for feasting and feeling grateful, but I was already feeling grateful that Carl hadn't swatted me with the wooden spoon from the kitchen drawer.

His eyes were red, as were my mother's. Joshua was wiping his nose. Luke sat calmly next to him. I couldn't speak but I also felt that my mother was ready to tell me the truth. Only she couldn't speak either.

Finally, when I thought the silence would make me crazy, Mother broke the quiet. Tapping me lightly on my shoulder, my mother began, "Sam...my dear Sam. I love you so much. When your father left I wasn't sure what I should tell you. I didn't want to lie, so I guess I decided to say nothing, thinking, I guess, that not saying anything wouldn't be a lie but would protect you."

I looked over at Joshua.

"I should let you know, first, that your daddy isn't in prison like you suspect."

"I know," I said, for I remembered very distinctly Joshua's words about Daddy's freedom. "He's out now."

My mother was silent, reviewing her thoughts. "Samantha, your father has never been in prison."

Joshua lifted his shoulders in doubt.

"But...but then where has he been?" I asked, looking past Joshua's eyes and turning to see the eyes of my mother.

Tears continued to crease her cheeks. "I'm sorry, Samantha. I'm so sorry I didn't tell you. Your father, well..." she looked over at Carl, I think for support, and then back at me and then briefly at my brother Luke.

"Your father has been very sick."

"What's wrong?"

My mind was reeling with thoughts of cancer and sicknesses that left you crippled and blind. If my daddy had been sick, a miracle had happened, and he was well now. And then an even sicker thought entered my mind. My daddy had been in a hospital for three years and I hadn't been able to even see him. Maybe he hadn't written or called because he'd been in a coma!

"Your father...has been in a special kind of place," Mother said.

"Where?" I asked.

"Riverdale Psychiatric."

"You mean a mental hospital?" My thoughts went quickly to June and then to all the places where the even crazier people went. But my daddy had never seemed crazy to me. Forgetful, yes, but not crazy.

June's comment about her aunt slitting her wrists sent a chill up my spine. Could Daddy have tried to kill himself?

"Your father has been sick for a long time," Mother was saying. "He stopped taking his medication."

I didn't even know my father was taking pills—well, except for vitamins.

"What kind of medication?" Luke asked. I'd almost forgotten that I wasn't alone in the room. Luke had scooted nearer to Carl, and Joshua was sitting on the other side of his father. They were still on the floor, but closer than when I'd first sat down. Interestingly, it made me feel secure for perhaps the first time in my life—other than the day Luke and Joshua had comforted me because I felt I had no one left who loved me.

"They helped him with his moods," Mother said.

I remembered all the times he was late with the milk or the bread, or the times he forgot to come home on time. Suddenly, it was like a picture was playing in my mind; it was a scary picture of lonely nights when he wouldn't come home until very late so we had to sit alone without him at the dinner table.

And then I remembered watching television with him and the closeness I felt as we watched one show after another. Daddy hadn't spoken then, but he'd held me close as if the words didn't matter.

"Where is Daddy now?" I asked.

"Living at his home," Carl said.

"Is his…wife still married to him?"

Mother seemed momentarily shocked. Carl smiled. "Yes, she is," he said, leaning closer in to me. Joshua and Luke stood near his chair, and Carl placed an arm around each waist, even though his arm didn't exactly fit all the way around Joshua's.

"Do you know how much we love you?" he asked.

Joshua and Luke nodded. They smiled, and I could see a piece of chocolate stuck in the side of Joshua's mouth.

I didn't nod. How could I? I wasn't sure about this love; I hadn't been sure since my mother's divorce. But had I known before then?

# CHAPTER 24

After sleeping in until noon, I woke to the thought of a beautiful butterfly landing within my heart. I walked into the kitchen.

"Mother, you didn't wake me up for school," I said, worried that she would be angry.

Instead she smiled and said, "Oh, you can miss one day."

I couldn't believe it. "Mother, are you sick?" I asked.

Snow had fallen the night before, great, huge globs that landed on cars and fences and roofs like the tops of ice-cream cones.

"I thought we should talk," Mother said, smiling. "I should have talked with you long before now."

"OK."

She placed a plate of scrambled eggs and two pieces of toast in front of me, and returned to the counter for another. I couldn't remember the last time I'd eaten breakfast in the afternoon, especially with my mother.

"Where's Joshua and Luke?" I asked.

"At school."

"You made them go?"

"No."

I couldn't figure it out. Why would two boys choose to go to school when they could be home goofing around?

My mother smiled. "I asked them to go. Told them I needed a day home with you."

"Really?"

My mother hesitated. I could almost see her thoughts working within her head like the insides of a clock. "I need to tell you something I don't believe your brothers are ready for."

"What?" I asked, taking a bite of egg and a gulp of milk.

My mother followed suit. She handed me a napkin from the middle of the table. "Milk moustache," she said.

I wiped my mouth.

"Your father wants to see you."

"I know," I said.

There was a moment's surprise in my mother's eyes.

"I've been spying," I said.

"Oh," my mother answered. "How long?"

"Since you married Carl."

"No, I mean how long have you known your father has been here?"

"Since I ran away."

Understanding filtered into my mother's eyes. "Is that why you thought your father was in prison, because of what Joshua thought?" I took another bite, trying not to meet her eyes. I could handle my mother being angry with me, but at Joshua?

"I'm sorry," my mother said. "It must have been terrible for you to hear that way."

"So when were you going to tell me?" I asked, trying to watch her brown eyes as she looked at me.

My mother hesitated and then reached across the yellow table. "You know I love you," she said.

"I guess," I answered, trying to look at her eyes but finding it difficult to do so.

"Oh, Samantha…you don't believe me, do you?"

Until the tears dropped from my eyes I hadn't realized I was crying. But suddenly my lunch eggs were swimming, like stones in a river.

"Oh, honey…" I pushed my chair back and stood to escape, but in a second my mother's arms were wrapped around me.

I sobbed a lot after that, soaking the top of my mother's shirt. When I was finished my mother said, "I'm taking you out."

We walked to the front room where almost everything terrible had happened in my life.

Outside, the snow was still falling like small puffballs. As my mother crossed to the driver's side of the car I got in on my own.

She smiled at me only once right before she started the car. But it was only after we were slowly making our way down the shoveled road that I remembered the eggs and milk still sitting on the kitchen table. For the first time that I could remember, my mother had forgotten to clean up.

* * *

"This is where your father and I met." We'd stopped right in front of what looked like an old store. There were at least five levels, with various colored bricks falling out in random spots. One window high above was missing. I couldn't help wondering what this place might have looked like when she'd met Daddy. Hopefully better.

"This was the finest dancing place on the planet," my mother said. "And your father was the smartest-dressed man I knew. We always met here, leaving our other dates stranded when we saw one another."

"You're kidding," I said, trying to imagine them doing this..

"He even proposed to me here."

I'd seen a picture of Mother and Daddy at their wedding, standing by the cake. He was skinny even then and her brown hair was short and curled nearer her cheeks. She wasn't smiling, just peacefully looking down at her cake as he held her.

"But you didn't get married here," I said, remembering the garden pictures in the wedding album she now kept hidden somewhere else.

"No. My mother wouldn't let us." She laughed. "It was an old building even then."

I laughed. And then my stomach growled.

"There is a small restaurant up there," she said pointing up the hill to a green building. "I haven't been to Rome since your father and I were dating."

She brushed the fine mist of snow from her coat. "Want to go?" she asked.

"Sure," I said, glad to get out of the cold for a moment. "But I thought Rome was far away from here."

"Only if you've forgotten to dream," my mother said.

# CHAPTER 25

Rome was even fancier than the Chinese restaurant Carl had taken me to. Each long table had a white tablecloth made of real fabric. All the way down the table there were shiny black chairs with fancy backs—and plenty of room, too.

When I sat down I could bend my elbows clear out and not even touch the chair next to me. Of course, I didn't want to bend my arms for long, because suddenly a waiter in black and white was filling the champagne glasses with water.

"Can I get you an antipasto, an hors d'oeuvre?" he asked.

My mother picked up the menu. "Ham and melon would be nice," she said.

"Very good, ma'am." The waiter left, and my mother smiled over at me.

It was almost one, and the restaurant was nearly full. There were men in business suits and women sitting with friends, gabbing quietly about their children. A song in another language was being played softly over my head. It sounded like Spanish, but it was probably Italian because of the name of the restaurant.

"What do you think?" my mother asked.

"It's…beautiful!" I said, looking to the wall of lights, dimmed to a soft glow. What looked like small palm trees sat in light brown containers, and nearby pictures of Rome offered a quick glimpse of the real place.

But it did feel like the real place, almost as if some magic wand had transported my mother and me clear across the world.

When the meal came I gasped at my plate. It was completely white, with a golden ring along the edges, and inside was something strangely beautiful. It was pizza cut in tiny rectangles, but not exactly pizza because the smell of the cheese was different from anything I had ever smelled before. The soft odor wafted up to my nose like the smell of spring, and I almost didn't want to take a bite it looked so wonderful.

But my mother smiled and took a bite of her own pizza. She'd used a fork to put a small piece into her mouth. I quickly discovered why. The crust was very thin, and very messy when I tried to lift it with my fingers, so I sat it back down on the glorious plate and took a bite of it with my fork.

The cheese on top was a straw yellow, and on the edges of the pizza there seemed to be leaves that could not be plucked off but were a part of the cheese itself. The taste was sweet and light and reminded me of sour cream.

"What did you say this was?" I asked my mother. I was totally and completely in heaven.

"Pizza gorgonzola."

"What's that?"

"You mean the gorgonzola?"

I nodded and took another bite of the delicious stuff.

"I believe gorgonzola is made in Molise. It comes out like the shape of a pear and has a small bump at the top."

"Where's Molise?" I asked.

"In Italy."

I'd only heard of Italy, of course, and so I remained silent for a time, tasting the wonders of some faraway land. It was my mother who finally broke my thoughts. "How about some white truffle?" she asked.

I looked across the table to see that she had finished. I'd heard of truffle before. "Isn't it kind of like chocolate?" I asked.

"It is chocolate," my mother answered. "A very special kind of chocolate."

A few moments later my mother had ordered the treat. Five minutes later the dessert was served. It came out on a similar white plate with a golden ring, only smaller. The truffles were thinly sliced and were almost translucent. I took a bite.

The sweet taste melted in my mouth. This was even better than the chocolate candy bars on Halloween.

My mother was smiling at me again. "Your father and I always loved it here." She paused and took another sliver into her mouth. Her eyes closed suddenly, as if she were dreaming of the chocolate or the last time she and Daddy had come here, or both.

Finally, she opened her eyes and looked at me. They seemed to be saying something about love and pain and love again. Could my mother really love me as much as she had said? Had I been stupid to believe anything else?

"When will I see Daddy?" I asked.

"Tomorrow. Is that too soon?" Mother didn't take another bite of truffle, even though one more was sitting on her plate.

"No," I answered. "I don't think so."

"Carl will be taking your brothers out," she said. "They won't know."

"Luke might want to know," I said. The truffle just melting within my mouth suddenly turned sour. I swallowed it.

"I know," my mother answered. "I don't plan on keeping it a secret for very long."

How long? I wondered. "I think you should tell him," I said.

"After tomorrow night," my mother answered. "I want you to see your father first."

* * *

I couldn't sleep. I had crazy dreams of Daddy and knives on the bed that he couldn't choose from. I could see him crying in the corner like Joshua's mother. I could see him choosing a knife like June's aunt. I wondered if I was crazy.

When the morning light drifted past my heavy eyes, I got up, dressed, and walked down the hall to call June. After June I'd call Bruce, and together we'd get through this. I knew they couldn't come with me, but I also knew that if I talked with them, I might feel better about the whole thing. At least, this was my hope.

I was almost to the yellow phone on the kitchen wall when my mother stopped me. "What's this?" she asked, holding up the blue book with the golden angel on it.

"It says right there." I pointed at the black letters that spelled out the words "Book of Mormon."

"Don't sass me," Mother said. "I want to know where you got it." She was wearing her robe with the orange and red flowers dancing across it. The tone of her voice scared me. It was as if we'd never talked yesterday. As if our hearts had never joined.

"Mr....Green," I croaked. "Why?"

"You know why, young lady. Do you know what book this is?"

I nodded, the stories of Nephi's family running through my mind like a fast-paced movie never wanting to finish. For I didn't want to finish with it—any of it. I was up to Second Nephi. I had decided, quite frankly, that I liked it.

"This...this book..." My mother beat it in the air over her head. "...this book is of the devil!"

"What?" I gasped, sure she was mistaken. What was the warmth I'd felt spreading through my veins as I'd read it? What was the glow in my heart, and the knowledge in my mind? Surely the devil couldn't cause that.

My mother's brown hair hung down her shoulders but, as yet, it hadn't been brushed. "Sit down," she directed.

I sat on the same chair as yesterday, thoughts of eggs and milk going through my mind like a movie you don't want to remember. My heart was beating fast. I didn't know what to do, but more importantly, I didn't know what to say.

My mother had words for both of us. "This book is the Bible of the Mormon church. Did you know that?"

I nodded, wondering to myself why Mother had allowed me to go to Tracey's baptism if she felt so strongly against it.

She seemed to read my mind. "I was pretty sure you would come home from that baptism a changed girl. Only you didn't return in the way I expected."

I wasn't sure at first what Mother meant. But my mother was explaining herself as if years of pain had been bottled up inside her and she had to let them out. "When I was just a bit older than you I had a Mormon tell me to leave the church."

"You went to the Mormon church?" I asked.

"I should have told you before. I should have prepared you for this. This woman...she told me that I stunk. She might as well have said, 'I'm better than you. You don't belong.'"

"You stunk?" I thought of a skunk and its accompanying smell.

"I smoked."

127

"Smoked cigarettes?"

"And other things."

I wondered what other things my mother could mean. She'd never smoked in the house. I'd never seen her smoke. Not once.

"If it hadn't been for Carl's prodding, you wouldn't have gone to that baptism and we wouldn't have had a need for this talk now."

I remained silent. Although I wanted to tell mother how I felt— the warmth that had entered my body as I'd watched Tracey's baptism, and how neat it had been to sit in Mr. Green's living room as he talked with me for the first time about the blue book with the angel on it—I just couldn't.

I looked up from the table to see Carl entering the room. "What's wrong?" he asked. "What have you done this time?"

But he didn't look as if he was asking me. He was looking down at the book.

# CHAPTER 26

"You've forgotten to dream," I said, repeating the same words my mother had said to me yesterday on our way to Rome.

My mother flinched.

"This…is not about dreams!" she said.

"How would you know? Have you read it?" I had sassed her and now she would punish me for sure. But Carl had taken the book away and he was flipping through the pages as if the book were merely a hand-held fan.

"I've heard of this book," he said, "but not in the way you are saying, honey." He handed the book back to me and gave me a smile.

"Have you finished it?" he asked.

"No."

"Do you want to?"

"Yes."

I looked over at Mother. Her lips were as tight as a sealed jar of pickles. She was speaking a thousand words with her eyes. But Carl's eyes were soft and surprisingly understanding.

"We'll talk about this later," he said. "After Samantha has finished with it."

My mother was surprised. Maybe she'd thought Carl would take it away, maybe even burn it. But instead he'd given it back to me as if it were the greatest prize in the world.

And maybe, just maybe, it was.

* * *

"And when ye shall receive these things, I would exhort you that you would ask God, the Eternal Father, in the name of Christ, if these things are not true; and if ye shall ask with a sincere heart, with real intent, having faith in Christ, he will manifest the truth of it unto you, by the power of the Holy Ghost. And by the power of the Holy Ghost ye may know the truth of all things..." (Moroni 10:3-5).

I placed the book on my bed with the page opened and walked down the hall. Something inside me felt strangely different, as if a new heart had suddenly been placed within my chest.

It was time for me to pray. The strange thing was—or maybe it wasn't so strange, but merely embarrassing—. "God is great; God is good; let us thank him for our food..." We hadn't even used those words at the dinner table, but I knew some people did.

This prayer had nothing to do with food anyway. How did you pray about a book? How would you know if you got an answer?

The book had said, "by the power of the Holy Ghost." But who was the Holy Ghost and what would the power feel like?

In the kitchen I picked up the phone. It was 5 P.M. I had spent the entire day reading in the Book of Mormon. Carl had brought me my lunch. Luke and Joshua hadn't bothered me once. And that was strange simply because they were always bothering me.

Tracey's voice was unmistakable. "Samantha, is that really you?" she asked.

"It's me," I said softly into the phone. "Can you meet me at the school?"

"I don't know if I can." Her voice was a little cold, and a bit rude, too; I felt as if a bee had just come up to me with a long stinger.

"Why? I mean—I have to ask you something."

"Ask me now. I'm babysitting."

"I can't. Please, Tracey..."

I don't know if it was my insistent tone of voice or my use of the word "please," but Tracey relented in that moment. "OK," she said. "I'll get my brother to watch the kids."

My mother only looked at me when I told her I was heading to the school. Carl smiled. "Be home by dinnertime," he said. "Your father is coming."

I nodded and retreated from the house with my thick coat around my shoulders and my muff covering my thin hands. It wasn't snowing today, but there were thick ice crystals hanging from the houses and the streets were as thick as an ice-skating rink. I decided not to take my bike.

At Mr. Green's house I stopped for a moment and looked in through the partially opened window. Mr. Green was sitting in a chair reading something. I could almost see him holding a book, maybe even the same one he'd given me. A warm glow rested within my heart although my cheeks were cold.

Turning the corner, I looked up at Mr. Grant's. The walkways were piled with snow—not even tire tracks made a pathway from the garage to the street—and I wondered about the day I'd found out the truth. For a moment I stood and watched the covered windows as if in that moment Mr. Grant would see me and wave. But of course that didn't happen, and I was left to wonder once again about Mr. Grant and the lonely life he lived.

June lived a few houses away, but I would have to travel down her street to see what she was doing, so I continued on, passing multi-colored brick houses and houses with aluminum siding. By the time I reached the school, I could see Tracey's perfect hair blowing in the chilling breeze. She was alone.

In two weeks it would be Thanksgiving. The visit with Daddy was tonight and I wasn't sure what to say to him. I wasn't even sure what I was going to say to Tracey.

# CHAPTER 27

"You look like the abominable snowman," she said.

I wiped the tears from my blue eyes and continued to the swing.

"Be careful. When you first sit down, it's like sitting on an ice cube."

She was right, but in a few minutes the cold had gone away, replaced by numbness. It was too cold to be swinging so I just sat there, thinking my own thoughts and allowing Tracey to do the same.

When the shivering began I knew I had sat still for too long, and so I pushed off. The cold stung at my cheeks and I could see my breath floating in the air like a cloud. Tracey had followed my lead. She was swinging opposite from me, our bodies flying like trapeze artists. Neither of us spoke.

And for a time we didn't need to. Perhaps the words would have ruined the warmth in my heart that cold day at the school. If I had spoken, perhaps, in the few moments of thought my answer wouldn't have been able to come. Or maybe I wouldn't have recognized it because I had been feeling it since leaving my house.

"How do you pray?" I finally asked, allowing my feet to slide to a stop.

For a moment I heard nothing, and then I could feel the cold air as Tracey stopped. Her eyes were clear green when she looked at me, and she was smiling.

"What a funny question."

I was suddenly embarrassed. I had asked the wrong thing. Now she would laugh.

"You don't know how to pray?"

"Well…no. Is that so bad?"

"No…I guess not. It's just…"

I looked away from Tracey's beauty and toward the mountains. They were solid white. I could no longer see a tree, but I knew they were there. Perhaps I should have just known how to pray. Maybe the secret was within me and I just couldn't see it.

Tracey had stood. She was tapping me on the arm. "Sam?"

"What?"

"I'm sorry."

"About what?"

"You know. I guess sometimes I think that because I know about something, everyone else knows about it too. But I didn't always know what I know now."

I looked into her eyes. They seemed to be pleading with me to understand. And I wondered, with all that beauty, how could Tracey really understand my heart? She probably never needed an explanation for anything.

Well, that wasn't exactly right. Halloween night we'd shared lots of things—and she'd told me stuff I'd had no idea about. I knew it scared her to ride bikes because of the death of her brother. A car had hit him and put him in a coma. Later he'd died, and her family wasn't the same for a long time. It was only after the missionary discussions that Tracey realized she would be able to see her brother again.

Tracey had already asked the question that was just now probing my heart; she was now a member of the church—and didn't you have to ask if the Book of Mormon was true in order to join the church?

"I just don't know what to do," I told her honestly. "Tonight, Daddy is coming to see me. I have to know if the Book of Mormon is true, but I don't know how to pray…"

"You've been reading the Book of Mormon?"

"I'm to the part about asking."

"You're in Moroni, Chapter 10?"

"Uh huh."

"You're kidding me, right?"

I didn't know what Tracey could mean. Why would I tease her about something so important?

"Mr. Green gave me the book a few months ago."

"I didn't know he was Mormon."

"He's not. But his wife was, I think. After she died Mr. Green read it. When I was over at his house one day he gave it to me."

"Wow. I mean, is it his wife's book?"

I smiled. "It even has some words in it written by her to her husband. He wasn't very excited about the book when she was alive."

"Oh." Tracey's words sounded final. She sat on the swing and looked up at the mountains. Wouldn't she ever tell me how to pray?

And then the words came, as if while looking up at the mountains the answer entered her mind.

"You kneel down," she said, "fold your arms, and close your eyes. You do this to show respect to Heavenly Father. Um...you may know him as God."

I nodded.

"Well, then you begin your prayer, 'Heavenly Father...' and you thank him for things."

"Like what?"

"Well, like...your family and friends. And then you ask him for what you want."

"Like a question?"

"Sure. Maybe you want help with your schoolwork. Or maybe you want to stop being angry at your brother. Or maybe you want to know if the Book of Mormon is true." She smiled and jumped off her swing. "Are you ready to pray?"

I nodded, the warmth of the book spilling over my soul like water. For a moment I remembered my mother's glass pitcher, the one I'd broken just before Daddy had left us, and in my mind I could see it mending as if it had never been broken.

"After you ask the question, just say, 'in the name of Jesus Christ, Amen.'"

"Is that all?"

"And then you wait for an answer."

"How will it come? Will I hear God's voice?" I asked.

"You might," Tracey said, placing her arm on my shoulder. A small tear had formed in the corner of her eye. She blinked and it was gone, dripping down her cheek and falling to her coat.

"Or you may feel warm inside. Or your back may tingle."

"I have already felt warm inside," I admitted.

Tracey grinned. "How do you feel now?" she asked.

"All warm, and like I can think without worry."

"What time is your dad coming?" she asked.

"About six."

"Are you scared?"

"A little."

"Maybe you should include that in your prayer, too. That you are scared and need Heavenly Father's help in talking with your father."

A few minutes later our conversation was over. I watched Tracey walk away, her perfect form getting smaller and smaller. And when I was alone I looked up at the mountains and thought of God. The snow was quickly seeping through my pants and chilling my knees. But I wasn't cold. I folded my arms and closed my eyes and began to pray.

# CHAPTER 28

"Heavenly Father…

"I thank you for my mother and Carl and my brothers. Sometimes I get mad, but I guess you know about that. I'm sorry for getting mad. I'm sorry I have been mean to Mr. Grant and my mother and to Carl who is trying to take care of me. Help my daddy. He is coming today…as you know. I'm scared. I'm afraid of him. Please help me…"

I could not mistake the warmth in my heart, and then a whispering of words came into my mind: "I am here."

I opened my eyes but saw no one. Only the white grass and the snow-covered mountains. I closed my eyes.

"Heavenly Father…is the Book of Mormon true?"

The calm was unmistakable. I could hear no cars, no screams of children playing in their yards. It was as if, just for me, God had allowed the quiet, just so I could hear him.

I waited only a moment, feeling the cold wind on my cheeks and the smell of pine from the trees. When the answer came it was as soft as a rose, as clear as the water dripping under the bridge at Bruce's house. I could not deny it, although it was but one word.

I stood and opened my eyes, wiping the tears that had seemingly frozen to my cold cheeks. Heavenly Father had given me an answer. And the answer was "yes."

\* \* \*

"Samantha!"

From a distance I could see someone walking toward me. The person was wearing a gray coat that fell almost to the ground. He was tall and his voice was deep like a man's.

My heart stopped, or it felt like it had stopped, and then it was beginning again like a quick-running wind-up toy. A few feet later I could see that it was a man for sure, and that he was smiling. But more important, I knew his smile.

"Daddy!"

I ran, stumbling over the hardened snow as if it was full of rocks, almost falling once, but catching myself just in time.

His arms were open before I'd reached him. They were warm and comforting and made me feel like nothing would ever go wrong again. I squeezed my daddy in a tight hug and felt his thin shoulders trembling. He was crying. We didn't speak; we only held one another until our tears had been replaced with joy.

"You've grown taller," he said at last, pulling me away from him.

"You're getting gray," I said.

He laughed. "Age before beauty."

I wasn't sure what he meant, only that if he was age I was probably beauty. I smiled. "I missed you," I said.

Tears welled up in Daddy's eyes. "I know," he said. "I've missed you too."

"I hear you've been to Rome." His arm was placed around my shoulders and we walked toward the parking lot.

I nodded, my mind flooding with warm memories. "What time is it?"

He stopped and pushed his sleeve up from his old gray coat. "Almost seven," he said.

"Seven!"

"Don't worry. Your mother told me where to find you."

"She's gonna kill me," I said.

Daddy took me in his arms. "Don't worry, Sam. She's not angry."

I looked over at the school parking lot but couldn't see Daddy's car.

"I left my car at the house." Warmth caressed my back, but I said nothing. "I thought it would give us some time to talk before saying good-bye to your mother."

"Where are you taking me?" I asked.

"Well…" He laughed just a little. "I thought Rome, but since your mother has already taken you…"

"Oh, but I'd love to go there!"

"Twice in one week?"

I nodded, my heart bursting within me.

"Alright then. Rome it is."

* * *

The waiter was a different one, but the feeling was the same. I had been transported across the world without even leaving my home state of Utah. And just like my mother had done, my father was staring at me with a grand smile, telling me how much he loved me.

I may have felt before that only I knew the complete truth, and that only I understood what was happening in my life, but I was wrong. There are many sides to one story, even though I believed my side was the only one.

Still, it was hard hearing Daddy's side.

"I needed to be in the hospital," Daddy was saying now. "I wouldn't take my medicine, and without my medicine I would see things, Samantha, things that weren't even there."

"Like what?" I couldn't help asking.

"Well, scary things. Things unreal. I'd tell you but I don't want to give you nightmares."

And so I told Daddy about the vampire who lived up the street who really wasn't a vampire after all—just an old man who needed help.

Daddy smiled and said, "What I saw was kind of like that."

"How did it happen?" I asked.

"I think it started out as stress. I was having a hard time at work. I was having a hard time being a husband to your mother. Later, I started to drink."

"Did you know Mother smoked?" I asked, and covered my mouth because I'd blabbed.

Daddy coughed. "No, I didn't," he said.

"She probably stopped before she met you," I offered.

"Probably. How is your mother anyway?"

"Happy," I said.

"That's good."

"Are you happy, Daddy?" I asked.

"I'm feeling better every day. How about you?"

The warm glow entered my heart once again. Actually, I was pretty sure it hadn't left even once since my prayer and seeing Daddy. But this much was for sure: I knew the Book of Mormon was true and that I wanted to be baptized. I knew that I could have an influence on Mr. Green and that he would join me on my special day. Perhaps one day he would be baptized too. I knew Carl would come and my daddy and maybe my mother. I hoped that Joshua and Luke wouldn't be noisy. I prayed that, after all, I had been right about Mr. Grant not being a vampire and that he wouldn't go around the room biting everyone's neck, because I knew in my heart that I needed to invite him too.

And of course there was June and Tracey. And Bruce. The love of my life. I would probably have to drag Bruce to the big event. He would probably tell me I was stupid or crazy or something. But he would come.

Tracey could help me know what to do, and June would want to sit on one of the front chairs, her red hair glistening, so that she could see me go under.

"You're deep in thought," Daddy said suddenly, and I realized I was eating my pizza without even knowing it.

"Sorry," I said.

"So what's been happening in your life?" he asked.

I wasn't sure where to start. When he left us? When I was angry because my mother wasn't telling me anything? When I found out that Mr. Green had a Book of Mormon in his house? Or maybe when I found out that Mr. Green was June's psychiatrist? Where did a girl begin when a father had been away for three years? What should she tell him? What thing would be the most important?

And suddenly, I knew. It was as if I was on my knees talking with God. The feeling of warmth rested within my heart and I could hear the comforting words being spoken in my mind: "I am here."

"Daddy...you broke my heart when you left me," I began. A small sob escaped my lips and I looked deeply into my daddy's eyes. We had the same eyes, bright blue. "But I'm feeling better now."

Today Daddy's eyes were a creamy blue, the color of Bear Lake on our last trip without him. But today he was with me. After three years of separation, he was taking me to dinner. It was a beginning.

I looked down and wiggled my toes underneath the table. It was like I could see beyond my shoes, directly to my bare feet and beyond them to the sandy beach. The currents were warm, the waves soft and flowing. In my mind I could see the round stones at the bottom of the water as if they were merely problems in my life— unresolved challenges sitting still waiting for me to toss them across the surface, like stones in a river. A river of stones.

# Acknowledgments

A warm thank-you to Diana Gourley, Rebecca Shelley and to my editor, Vicki Schmitz.

# About the Author

Before Kathryn was one, she loved to read books—or at least pretend to. She couldn't walk yet but would crawl to the bottom shelf to get what she wanted. Her grandma says that Kathryn's books were placed near the floor for that very reason, and her mother remembers Kathryn pulling her favorite book from the shelf and crawling back to the couch, the book safely in tow. Sitting on the couch, Kathryn would pretend to read, speaking the language of some foreign diplomat—or, perhaps, the tongue of angels (her mother wasn't quite sure which)—and when she was done, Kathryn would crawl back to the shelf for another story.

When Kathryn isn't writing she is reading. A member of the Church of Jesus Christ of Latter-day Saints (Mormon), she is an avid reader of the scriptures and books of spiritual merit. She is married and enjoys teaching and working with youth and children—including her own three girls.

Kathryn has been a published writer since 1987; her work includes various newspaper and magazine articles for teens and adults. *A River of Stones* is her first novel.

www.ingramcontent.com/pod-product-compliance
Lightning Source LLC
Chambersburg PA
CBHW050900180626
46814CB00007B/2809